Karen L. Syed

Lost and Found

Lost and Found
An Echelon Press Book

First Echelon Press Publication 2001
Second Echelon Publication January 2012

Echelon Press
2721 Village Pine Terrace
Orlando, FL 32833
www.echelonpress.com

ISBN 978-1-59080-856-6

Published by Echelon Press LLC.

This book is especially dedicated to Moghis. His unwavering support in all my adventures is truly inspiring.

◀ One ▶

"Leave it to Mother Nature."

Lightning flashed across the darkened sky, immediately followed by a deep roll of thunder. Allison Ryder turned the key in the ignition of her precious classic 1965 Mustang and the engine roared to life. She reached forward with trembling fingers and flipped the windshield wiper switch.

"Oh, would you look at that," Allison said, annoyed by the gold-colored paper swishing back and forth across the front window of her car.

"Settle down. It's just a flyer," Katie consoled.

"I know what it is." Allison snapped at her best friend as she stumbled back into the downpour. "Lord, I hate Texas storms."

With the icy cold rain pelting down onto her head, she reached to snatch the flyer off her windshield; or tried to. The swish of the rubber blade pulled the paper out of her reach and then tormented her by tossing it, along with a stream of water, back at her. A moment too late, she figured it probably would have been easier if she'd turned the wipers off first. The blade snapped back toward her again and sent another stream of water directly at her face. "Crud!"

She finally ended up with a wad of wet paper stuck to her fingers. Infuriated by the whole situation, she jumped back into the car and shook her hand, trying to get the soaked paper loose. It landed on top of one of the bags settled in the back seat.

Once a week she made the trip into the heart of town to buy groceries and every week someone stuck one of those stupid flyers on her car. According to the numerous advertisements, she could lose twenty pounds in twenty hours. She could find Mr. Right through her VCR. Heck, she could even increase her annual salary by one hundred times by simply using her home computer. With all the wonders of the flyer world, her life should be perfect. "I hate it when they do this in the rain. Don't they know what a mess they make? What right do they have?"

"They should all be shot at dawn." Katie said from the passenger seat, her green eyes sparkling and a knowing grin spread across her face. "To hell with free enterprise and all that stuff."

"Oh stop patronizing me," Allison snapped playfully.

"What did I say? I'm just voicing an observation on your behalf."

Katie turned her head away and Allison reluctantly smiled as her friend's rosy cheek twitched. "You might as well laugh, before you explode. Lord knows I don't want your twisted sense of humor splattered all over my nice leather seats."

"Oh that's sick, Al."

Allison grinned. "Oh yeah, like you aren't, giggle girl."

"Not me. I have absolutely no desire to laugh at you." Katie snorted.

"What kind of person has so much time on their hands they can walk around tormenting people with useless pieces of paper?"

Katie pushed her overly long brown curls out of her eyes and sniffed. "What kind of person lets a piece of paper ruin her day?"

Allison glanced over the back of her seat and stretched to see around the van parked next to her. Not seeing anything, she stepped on the gas and the car rolled slowly backward. "You just don't get it. Someone had to cut down trees to make the paper this is printed on."

"It happens," Katie acknowledged.

"Then someone pollutes the air with all the machinery that makes and prints the paper."

"And this is what's got your knickers in such a twist? For heaven's sake, Al, plant a tree." Katie settled into her seat and checked her seatbelt as the car started to back up.

Thud!

Al's foot went instinctively to the brake pedal and the car jerked to a stop. Staring into her rearview mirror, she looked through the rain smatterings into a very deep, brown pair of eyes glaring in at her. A split second later, she noticed the man the eyes belonged to, leaning half up on the trunk of her car. She slammed the car into park and jumped out into the rain. Thank God she hadn't been moving fast enough to hurt him.

"Why me, Lord?" she mumbled.

He raised head up and the hood of his rain jacket slipped back. Dark hair hung, dripping around his face.

His angry gaze locked on her and she fought the urge to step back. "Oh my."

"What are you trying to do, kill me?" he shouted.

She stared, mesmerized as the creases across his tanned forehead deepened.

"Hel-lo. Anybody in there?" he asked sarcastically.

Allison could barely hear him over the car's engine and the rain, but he didn't sound happy.

"I'm sorry. I looked and didn't see anyone. Are you okay?"

"Yeah, fine for someone who just almost got run over by a crazy woman driver. Didn't anyone ever tell you cars can kill people if you don't know how to drive them?"

"I just couldn't see around the van," Allison offered, apologetically. The man turned to walk away and she noticed the hood of his plastic jacket sagging from the weight of rainwater quickly filling it up.

Large cold drops fell onto her head, dripping down her face as she shook her head against the chills. Her damp collar sagged against her neck. Still disquieted by his intense stare, Allison looked around her. Several cars drove past, splashing muddy water up onto their legs.

The irritated man shook his leg and mumbled in her direction. "If you couldn't see, you shouldn't have gone." He turned back and glared at her.

"That makes no sense. I would have had to wait until the owner of the van came out. Perhaps you should have looked to see if my reverse lights were on."

"Well forgive me; I had other things on my mind." He pushed his hair back and reached for his hood.

She opened her mouth to warn him about the water, but he held up a hand to silence her.

"Don't tell me, let me guess."

She tried again to speak, but he went on without giving her a chance to say anything else.

"You're sorry. Do you know how many people are killed by careless drivers who have no business out driving in the rain?"

His eyes turned dark and something sad flashed across his features, but the anger quickly returned. Rain dripped down inside her jacket, drowning what little patience she had left and she decided he could use a good cooling off. "Actually, I wanted to tell you . . . oh, never mind." She stifled the nervous giggle threatening to erupt from inside her. "Do you want my name and address or anything?"

He stared at her. "Why? So we can date?"

This man's arrogance riled her and she struggled harder to hold her tongue. "In case you're hurt."

"No. I'm fine. Just try to be careful in the future. I'm still young and I'd like to live long enough to grow old."

The sadness returned to his features. Allison offered him a weak smile and climbed back into the car. She looked back in time to see him flip his hood back onto his head and a wave of water wash down over his face and into his eyes. She turned her head away so he couldn't see her smile. She strained to hear the faint rumblings of his curses as he ran off.

"Is he okay, Al?" Katie asked.

"Yeah, he says he is. What else can go wrong today?"

"You okay?"

"Sorry, I'm just having a bad week." That's a gross understatement, Allison thought.

"So I see. Want to tell me about it?"

How could she tell Katie the most important thing in their life was about to become non-existent? She'd rather roll in a fire ant bed than be the bearer of bad news. "Just forget it."

"Fine."

"Okay." Allison stared straight ahead in silence.

She could feel the wrinkles on her forehead and reminded herself not to frown so much. She made a mental note to buy the economy size jar of skin cream on her next trip to the drug store. The inevitability of wrinkles gave her less and less reason to smile, which meant if she weren't careful she'd end up looking like a raisin.

Years of living under the Texas sun had taken their toll on her mother and once they'd diagnosed the cancer it had been too late to save her. Allison shook off the image of her mother's wrinkled and battered skin against the stark white pillows of her deathbed.

"Allison, do you have any recollection of how to have fun?"

Allison slowly turned and faced her friend. "And what the heck does that have to do with anything?"

"Everything," Katie replied.

"Like?"

"I can't remember the last time I saw you smile and you never go out with us anymore. I'm worried about you."

"Well don't be. I've just been busy. Things aren't good at the shelter."

"What do you mean, Al?"

Dang. She hadn't meant to say that. Allison knew the moment of truth had arrived and she hated having to be the one to tell. Katie cared about very few things outside her family and one of them was about to be destroyed.

"I think Doc is gonna close the shelter." She saw the surprised look on Katie's face and knew she'd have to explain.

"What do you mean, you think? Either he is, or he isn't. How could he? Where will all those poor babies go?"

Allison hated to even think about it. "I don't know. He says he's too old to do it anymore and wants to go live in Utah with his son."

When Katie sighed, Allison realized they were

still sitting in the parking lot. She shifted the car into reverse, carefully slipped the Mustang out of the parking space, and headed for home. When she turned her head to look at her best friend she noticed the worry lines on Katie's forehead. Maybe they could save money if they bought wrinkle cream in bulk. She brushed a stray lock of deep auburn hair away from Katie's face.

"You okay about this, Honey?"

"Yeah, fine." Katie sighed.

Allison knew she wasn't, but couldn't think of any words of comfort. Katie meant the world to her and she hated seeing her upset. She'd been wonderful to her since she'd come back to Texas.

Brasselton, Texas was a small town. Most of the world didn't even know it existed. Ten years earlier, a freak storm had whipped a series of tornadoes through and destroyed most of the town. Some of the residents who'd lost their homes didn't have the money, or desire to rebuild, so they'd packed up and left. Many had left behind family pets of one variety or another. Katie, unable to bear the thought of all those *poor babies* alone and hungry, started taking them in.

A year later, Allison had dropped out of college and moved back to Brasselton to care for her ailing mother. Unable to find work as a veterinary assistant, she'd gone to work in a dog-grooming salon. That's how she'd met Katie. She brought the strays in to have them cleaned up.

Then she'd opened Katie's Care Shelter and Salon,

a home for wayward strays. Allison had liked Katie immediately and they'd become great friends. The dog groomer had reluctantly let Al go when Katie asked her to work for her. They'd worked side by side until Katie got pregnant with Justin. Her husband had all but forbidden her to continue with her work. His fear of her contracting some disease from a stray animal had led him to force the issue of safety. So, she'd sold the business to Doc MacGruder, who'd run it for going on six years. Now he planned to close it down.

"I don't know what to do, Katie."

"It's not your problem, Al." Katie continued to stare out the window.

"Look, I hate this as much as you, but it's not either of our business to handle."

Katie turned sideways in her seat, her face suddenly beaming with enthusiasm. "But it could be."

That expression always led to the same talk. "Oh no! We've been over this a hundred times before. I don't have the money or the–" Allison stopped when she saw Katie's eyes twinkling.

"The what? The time." Katie rolled her eyes and heaved an exaggerated sigh. "You've got nothing but time. And if Doc closes you'll be unemployed."

"Hel-lo! Un-em-ployed. Does that word mean anything to you? Of course not, you have a husband to spoil and support you. If I'm unemployed where would I get money to buy and run an animal shelter?"

"Allison, stop whining and listen to me."

Allison watched her friend's animated hand

gestures and the melodrama with which she pleaded her case.

"I'm not whining, I'm complaining. There's a difference."

"Whatever. Anthony would do anything for me."

"Well, I'm glad you shared that. I feel much better about the condition of my life now." Allison maneuvered the car around the corner and headed down the road toward her house. "Maybe I would understand better if I had someone who'd do anything for me."

"What if I ask him to help me–us–buy it back?"

"Katie, you know how he feels about you working. He'd never let you do it."

"He would if I told him we would be partners and you were going to run it."

Allison turned and stared at her friend.

"Allison, look out!"

The sound of a truck horn blaring pulled her attention back to the road. She swerved in time to avoid crossing the centerline. The man driving the pickup truck in the oncoming lane graced her with a colorful hand gesture.

"Katie, you can't be serious. Look at what you do to me. All this hooey you're spewing almost got us killed." Several more cars passed them as Allison carefully made her way home. She swerved to miss several puddles of water that she knew as potholes in disguise. She had no intention of bottoming her baby out. She tried to ignore Katie's rambling by considering how much it would cost to repair the Mustang. Parts weren't cheap.

"Why not? By the way, I'm not the one driving. This is a great idea."

"Oh my. You are serious." Allison slowed and pulled the car up next to the curb in front of her house. The rain splattered against the windshield and she considered leaving the groceries in the car, but decided to save the innocent lives of her ice cream and milk. She cared too much for the classic car she'd inherited from her mother to let melted treats ruin the original upholstery. Katie sat staring straight ahead–pouting.

Allison began gathering up her bags. With several plastic sack handles cutting into her fingers she turned toward Katie. "Are you gonna help me?"

"Oh, I see. I ask a favor, you say no, and then you ask for a favor and expect me to say yes." She shook her head and made clicking noises with her tongue; the same noise Allison had fallen victim to when Katie had first asked her about going to work for her years earlier.

"Oh stop it. I didn't say no. I just don't think Tony will go for it."

"Does that mean if he will, you'll do it?"

Allison tucked her hands onto her hips. "Oh for Heaven's sake."

"It would help assure that you never have to worry about being unemployed and we'd be partners." Katie fidgeted in her seat, barely able to contain her excitement.

"If I say yes, will it get you and my ice cream into the house?"

Katie rubbed her chin and with a victorious grin nodded her approval. "Fine, we can go in now."

They jumped out of the car and pulled the bags of food from the back seat. Allison tossed her keys to Katie and watched her run toward the house. She was about to close the car door when she saw the crumpled up flyer. She grabbed it off the seat and slammed the car door.

She made it half way across the yard before she saw the soaking wet ball of fur with a pink bandanna wrapped around its neck running toward her. The golden retriever jumped around her feet, nipping playfully at her bags.

"Stop it. Go home." She stepped sideways to avoid a collision with the dog, but the strange pup jumped in front of her. She was familiar enough in general with dogs to realize it didn't want to hurt her. The animal simply wanted to play. As cute as she was, the middle of a rainstorm was not the time.

"Allison, what are doing?" Katie stood under the protection of the porch roof motioning her to hurry up. "Stop playing with the dog and get up here before you catch a chill."

"Brilliant idea, Katie. Tell it to the pup." Allison stopped to give the dog a chance to see she wasn't playing. "Okay, you go home now and we can play later. Go on."

Droplets of water rolled down her forehead. The

mixture of conditioning mousse and rain burned her eyes and she squinted against the stinging sensation. The dog stopped and leaned forward, barking cheerfully. She looked terribly comical with her front paws stretched out in front of her and her tail up in the air wagging furiously. Water shot through the air from the sweeping motion of the dog's tail and Allison couldn't help but laugh.

"Okay, enough is enough. Go home so I can get in the house." Allison made a dash for the house. She'd moved almost five feet when she heard the squeal and the earth disappeared out from under her.

The slippery plastic bags slid out of her hands only seconds before she hit the ground. Every bone in her body vibrated and she thought she might have swallowed several of her teeth.

Allison lay still on the wet grass with her eyes closed.

Carefully, she took several deep breaths hoping to get some air into her lungs, but there was none to be had. It wasn't until Allison opened her eyes that she realized the reason she couldn't breathe had a lot to do with the huge sopping wet dog sitting on top of her.

"Get off me." She gasped.

She raised her head to see Katie pulling the stray dog off. "Would you stop playing and get up. You'll catch your death wallowing in that puddle."

She stood up and brushed some of the loose grass off her soaking wet bottom while Katie led the dog to the shed.

Katie came back several minutes later and helped her pick up the last of the groceries.

They didn't hurry to the house since they were both drenched anyway. Once Allison got into the kitchen, she plopped down into the closest chair.

"Oh, Al, are you okay?" Katie kept her head down and didn't look directly into Allison's face.

"I'm fine. Nothing a few months of physical therapy and some counseling won't take care of." She took several deep breaths. "And don't you dare laugh." Moments later, her anger slipped away, and her breathing returned to normal. "I swear you have spent the entire day laughing at me."

"I didn't even see her. Who does she belong to?"

"I wish I knew. I've never seen her before either, but I sure would like to know."

"Hey, what's that in your hand?"

Allison looked down and realized she still clutched the flyer. "That's it, the dang flyer is cursed." She opened her hand and smoothed it down onto the table, trying to match up the torn edges. "I'd like to know what is so all fired important that they had to ruin my life with one piece of paper."

"Uh huh, me too." Katie stood behind her and laughed.

"Oh, it's not that funny."

"Yes, it is, Al."

Allison read it aloud. "Lost! Large enthusiastically playful golden retriever puppy. Please contact–"

"Oh, Allison, you're a hero."

"Puppy my foot. That beast is *Cujo*'s sister."

"But she loves you," Katie argued playfully. "I could tell by the way she watched you as I dragged her to the shed. I could barely keep her from running back to you."

"I've lived this long without love; I could have continued to survive without it."

Allison tossed the flyer down on the oak table and got up to put her groceries away. When she reached for the bag across the table, a sharp twinge of pain in her lower back stopped her. She straightened up and rubbed the spot.

"You okay, Al?" Katie stared at her waiting for an answer, concern etched in her features.

"I think I must have twisted my back when I fell over *Marmaduke*."

"You aren't blaming that poor puppy are you? I think you should call her owners and take it out on them."

"What's the flyer say?" Katie picked up the bright gold piece of paper and read the bottom. "Hey, it gives this street as an address."

"That can't be right. I know everyone on this street."

"Maybe you have new neighbors."

"Oh, Katie, come on. The only house on the street that's vacant is the one on the corner. The Town Council has been threatening to tear it down for years."

"Why haven't they?" Katie asked.

"Someone from out of town keeps stopping the

paperwork. Something about it being a landmark."

Katie moved over to the back door and stepped out onto the porch. The dark clouds drifted past as the rain lessened. Allison moved to stand behind her and breathed in the fresh scent. "Is that the house over there?" Katie pointed toward the end of the street.

"Yep, it's more of an eyesore than anything." She pulled her attention away from the old house. Allison rested her chin on Katie's shoulder and together they watched the sun slip down behind the trees.

"I'm so glad I moved back to Texas. I've never seen a sunset even close to this beautiful." Allison draped her arm around her friend's shoulder and they watched the brilliant colors blaze across the big sky.

"Al, I think you should call the number on the flyer. They might be worried."

"Yeah, I'll bet *Marmaduke* has already trashed my shed." Allison picked up the flyer and searched for the name and telephone number.

"Oh my. What the heck kind of name is that?"

"Wilfred Hoyt. I can only imagine what he looks like. I can just see some poor old man in coveralls, half crippled and hunched over trying to keep track of that heathen." Allison laughed.

"Hey, girlfriend, maybe you can get a date out of this."

Frowning at her friend, Allison sighed. "What is it about this day that everyone who speaks to me thinks I should be dating?"

"I beg your pardon? You mean I'm not the only

one who thinks you spend too much time playing *Dr. Doolittle*? This man could turn out to be a real hottie."

Allison smacked playfully at her friend and they laughed. "Yeah, Wilfred sounds like a heck of a stud."

"Just call so you can get rid of your house guest. She sounds like she's getting impatient." They stopped talking and listened to the dog barking and yipping into the now quiet evening. "At least the storm has passed and they can come get her sooner."

Allison picked up the cordless telephone and dialed the number.

The chipper voice that answered only added to her irritation. She explained the situation then wrapped up the call. "Well, just give him the message with my address and tell him I have his dog. I'll be home all night."

Allison shoved the telephone into the base and leaned against the counter. The last thing she wanted was to be saddled with the horse of a dog for the night. There were reasons why she didn't bring her work home with her.

"Well, Al, I don't know about you, but I'm hungry."

"Me too, but I need to shower before I do anything. Can you wait?"

Katie waved a hand at her and smiled. "Yeah, I've got all night. Tony took the wee one to Grandpa's for the night. They're going fishing in the morning. I can stay as late as I want."

"Hey, why don't you stay the night? It's been years

since I had a sleep over."

"Only if we can order pizza and I get the fluffy pillow."

"You're on. I'll be down in a minute. You go ahead and order dinner while I shower."

Allison stood in the shower letting the steaming hot water roll off her into the bathtub. The throbbing in her back had gotten worse, but the heat from the water helped ease some of the tension. She was looking forward to facing the old coot who owned the dog. She had a juicy piece of mind to give him.

She heard the doorbell ring just as she turned off the blow dryer. She looked in the mirror, picking at her roots as she pulled the comb through her dark brown hair one last time. "Looks like it's time for another date with Miss Clairol," she said to her reflection. *What are they all talking about? I date.* Allison fluffed her bangs and turned off the light. She wanted to get downstairs to pay for the pizza before Katie could. Katie never let her pay for anything.

"I've got it, Katie." When Allison reached the bottom of the staircase, she found the foyer empty. She went into the kitchen and found nothing. "Where'd ya go?"

"I'm out back," Katie shouted from outside. "Wilfred came to pick up his dog."

Allison stepped off the back porch and headed toward her shed. Carefully, she sidestepped several puddles she knew covered holes in her yard. She rounded the corner of the house and saw Katie open the door to the shed. She caught a glimpse of a man next to her as he bent over. She raised her hand to wave, and then she saw it. Everything bad in her life flashed before her eyes, in slow motion no less.

"No!" Everyone shouted at once.

Before she could stop the impending doom, it slammed into her chest at full force and knocked her to the ground. Cold and musty smelling mud seeped up around her and soaked through her clean clothes. She bit down hard on her lower lip, what was left of it, holding back the string of curses that would surely lose her a spot in heaven.

Nothing made sense. Small goose bumps of annoyance rose on her arms as a warm tongue slid up her face. As she lay on the ground, she prayed for the patience to not strangle the dog, or its owner.

"Al, honey, are you all right?"

The sound of Katie's voice rang in her head, but it wasn't her friend she saw when she finally got her eyes open. She stared up into very deep, very brown– "Oh my."

"Howdy neighbor."

◀ Two ▶

Ebony lashes framed his smoldering eyes. His high cheekbones and squared jaw screamed to be caressed. Why hadn't she noticed how handsome he was when she'd nearly run over him in the grocery store parking lot? "Oh my."

"Are you hurt? Should we call the doctor?"

"I'm not–" Blood began to pound in her temples, as she lay on the ground in total denial of what might prove to be her most humiliating moment.

"Can you stand up?" Just a hint of concern tinged his question. His dry clothes and bright expression were a definite contrast to the disgruntled man she'd *met* earlier.

The combination of his husky voice and chocolate brown eyes should be outlawed. She forced her eyes open wide enough to watch him pull the dog away from her. Then again maybe not. Why waste a good thing. The slap of wet fur on her face brought back her irritation.

"Oh, Al, let me help you up." Katie shoved her way between the dog and Allison.

The painful ache in her back loosened the reins on Allison's temper. "Oh sure. We can have a T-shirt made up for me that says I survived the sequel."

Katie stifled a giggle and stepped back.

"Don't you dare laugh at me, Katherine Kay."

"Hey, I'm really sorry. This is all my fault." The stranger stepped forward. "Wait, the sequel? I'm confused."

The hand he extended toward her fit perfectly around hers as he pulled her up. She stared at his fingers. Perfect. Not too soft, but no horrible disfiguring scars. Neatly trimmed nails, with just enough dirt under them to prove he worked with his hands.

Allison stood in the middle of her yard dripping mud and mad as a wet hen. It wasn't until she'd wiped the last traces of mud from her eyes that she took a good long look at the beast's owner. Too bad someone so irresponsible and inconsiderate looked so good, and so concerned. Then again who was she to call him irresponsible? She'd used her car and not a dog to do her handy work.

"Allison and the puppy met earlier and Al ended up on her back. Similar to now."

"She must really like you." Small dimples appeared in his cheeks as he struggled to hold back a grin.

Allison couldn't stand the thought of being attracted to this–man. "Bully for me," she snapped, venting some of her anger at herself.

Allison wished at that very moment she'd gone with her friends to the self-defense classes in college.

She would have flipped this guy into next week, just because he was so damn good looking. What right did he have? Torn between anger and awe, she lifted her hand to shake his, stud muffin or not. He looked down and frowned at the mud dripping off it. Annoyed by his obvious reluctance and feeling more than a little petty, Allison grabbed his hand and pumped it–hard. The motion sent several globs of mud onto his blue Oxford shirt.

He pulled his hand away and hesitated. He finally shook it off and let it hang down by his side. "I'm just glad I'm alive to be here." He grinned and Allison noticed a glint of humor in his eyes.

"Lucky us."

"I really am sorry. We thought we had her secured, but she can be a real handful at times." The dog jumped around in the puddles beside them. A continuous stream of mud splashed out from under her massive paws. Every few seconds, the pup nuzzled up to Allison's hand.

"No kidding," Allison said sarcastically, as she petted her head.

"Allison, be nice. He's come to take the puppy home." Katie had a heart of gold and Allison knew her friend was trying to save the stranger from the tongue-lashing they all knew he deserved.

"Great. I hope you'll tell your grandfather to keep a better eye on his pet."

"Uh, Allison, I don't think you understand."

Allison, held up her hand, interrupting Katie

before she could go on. "As you've already said, a dog like this can be a real handful."

"Allison–"

"Katie, please." Allison stepped toward the man and looked up into his eyes. "If you don't mind my saying so, I think a smaller pet would be more appropriate for an older man."

"An older man?"

She stopped talking when the man's face expressed confusion. "Well, yes."

"Allison," Katie interrupted. "I'd like you to me Mr. Hoyt."

He smiled.

"Mr. Wilfred Hoyt." Katie said insistently.

"Nice to meet you, Mr.–" She listened with bewilderment. She would have to remind herself to amend that embarrassing moment thing from earlier. Allison stammered and searched for words. "You're– you can't–"

"Wilfred Hoyt. That's me."

"But you're not old and hunched over," Allison choked out. "Oh my."

"Thank you for noticing. I do have my good days."

Allison had stepped into a big pile of it and her squirming decidedly amused the man in front of her. She couldn't ignore the seriously bruised feeling of her pride as they both stared at her.

"Allison?"

"Not now, Katie. I'm not finished making a total fool of myself."

"Oh?" was all Katie said.

"I assumed from your name that you were–oh my."

"My grandfather?" he questioned.

"Well, yes."

"I hope you're not disappointed."

"No not at all. I mean, yes. I mean–"

His eyebrow arched in surprise and his lips curved up into a mischievous grin. "I'm glad I'm not him."

"Why's that?"

"He died two years ago."

"Oh my."

"You said that. Several times in fact." He turned to Katie, who offered him an apologetic shrug. He laughed aloud. A deep genuine laugh. "I believe your friend is finished now."

Allison stood speechless as he leaned down and took hold of the dog's collar. The sound of his laughter ringing out into the night sent chills along her spine.

"Hoyden and I will be going now. It's been a pleasure meeting you. Say goodnight, Hoyden."

Ruff!

She waited for him to cross the street before she picked up a handful of mud and flung it in his direction. Not her finest, or most mature moment, but it kept her from screaming in humiliation and frustration.

"I saw that," he called back.

Allison cringed.

* * *

"What a spitfire she is, huh, Hoyden?" Will Hoyt led the dripping retriever across the street and into his own yard. He maneuvered his rambunctious pet into the fenced area behind his house and looped the chain through her collar. "She's pretty though, huh?

Ruff ruff! Hoyden yipped happily at his heels as he stepped away. Before Will could get out of her line of fire, she jumped up on his back and slammed her tongue against the back of his neck. He jumped forward and Hoyden danced around him playfully.

"Dang it, Hoyden. I didn't pay all that money for obedience school so you could keep ruining my shirts." The mud from her soppy paws soaked through the cotton fabric and he shivered. He twisted around trying to catch a glimpse of how seriously destroyed his shirt was. Feeling, oddly enough, like a dog chasing his own tail, he straightened around and stared at Hoyden. "Did you see that? I'm starting to act like you, and quite honestly I'm not pleased by that revelation."

He smiled when the overzealous puppy plopped down right in the middle of a puddle.

"Why do you keep sitting in puddles? You're supposed to be a lady."

She stared up at him with the most exasperating, pitiful face he'd ever seen.

"Oh, you're all right. I'm not mad at you." Will stooped down and offered his hand to her. Ignoring his peace offering, she bounded forward and knocked him to the ground. With a splash, Will landed on his bottom in a puddle.

He heard the stifled giggle from near the house, and turned to look. His fifteen-year-old niece, Lizzie, stood on the side doorstep.

"Is that you, Uncle Will?" she asked as she walked toward him.

"Yeah, it's me and the beast. What are you doing outside?"

"I heard a noise and wanted to make sure it was you." She casually strolled down off the porch and stopped above him.

Will flung his hands up into the air and sighed. "You thought there was a prowler so you came outside alone?"

He accepted her hand and with help from the girl, he extracted himself from the affections of the dog and the oozing of the puddle. After several sweeps of his hands across the seat of his trousers, he declared the entire day a disaster. With any luck, the mud would wash out. He shoved his hands into his pockets and walked toward the steps.

"I heard you talking to Hoyden, so I came out to see if everything was okay. Just in time, I'd say."

"Lizzie, you need to be more careful. What if I had been a prowler?"

"I'm not a baby, Uncle Will."

That's for sure, he thought looking at her. A fifteen-year-old blessed–or cursed, depending on how you looked at it–with the body of a twenty-year-old. He looked from Lizzie to Hoyden and realized he'd have his hands full with the two of them. He opened the door leading into the kitchen.

Will draped his arm around her shoulder and smiled. "I know, Lizzie, but you're all I have left and I want to make sure you stay safe."

Will thought about his sister, Marty. They'd always been close and he missed her. Two years seemed like a long time, but how long would it really take to get over the loss of a sibling?

"You thinking about Mom?" Lizzie took his hand and pulled him into the house. "I miss her."

Will struggled to keep his smile in place. "Yeah, kiddo. I miss her a lot, too. However, I feel a lot closer to her with you here. I only wish you hadn't waited so long to come live with me."

Lizzie sighed and plopped down into a kitchen chair. "I know, but Aunt Grace thought it was best if I stayed with them until you got settled. I think she had a hard time letting go of Dad. She needed me there."

Will turned away so she couldn't see his frown. Yeah, they kept you long enough to find out your folks didn't leave them anything, he thought.

"I know you don't like Aunt Grace, but she was real nice to me."

"I know, kiddo." He handed her the glass of orange juice he'd just poured and smiled. People could always be nice when they thought they were going to inherit a fortune.

"Uncle Will, can we talk?" He glanced up at her and the expression on her face reminded him of Marty. Lizzie wore the same expression her mother always wore when she wanted something.

"I guess," he answered warily.

"I was going through my closet and just between you and me I think I need some new clothes."

"What's wrong with the ones you have?" Most of what he'd seen her wearing looked fine. In fact, Lizzie was one of the best-dressed kids in the world. He should know; he'd spent a small fortune on a lot of it.

"Well, the clothes I have just don't seem right for a small town like this. I need to fit in."

"You will."

"No, Uncle Will, I won't. My clothes are for the city. You know, afternoons at the club and all those parties. I need country clothes."

"Well, I don't know anything about the latest fashions or anything. Can't you go pick out a few things in town?"

She tossed her hands up in the air and flung herself across the table, a scene worthy of an Academy Award. "Have you seen the rags they're trying to pass off as clothes?"

"What's wrong with them? I bought a couple of outfits the other day and they're fine."

"Oh good golly! You're a man. You don't care what you look like." She frowned at him when he laughed.

"I beg your pardon. I do so care what I look like. Hey, I let you talk me into this earring, didn't I?" He fingered the small stud in his ear and flinched from the tenderness.

"Oh, men will wear anything. I'd hoped maybe we could go into–"

The front doorbell interrupted her sentence and she gave him a melodramatic sigh. She didn't move from her seat.

Will stood up and laid his hand on Lizzie's shoulder. "No, it's okay, Lizzie. I'll get it."

"Okay," she said smiling at him with all the sincerity he figured a fifteen-year-old could muster.

"Brat." Will returned her smiled as he walked out of the room. Stepping over several piles of crumpled newspapers, he weaved his way through a maze of half-unpacked boxes to get to the front door. He saw the shadow through the frosted glass, but couldn't see who stood on the other side. He pulled the door open.

"Hi."

Allison Ryder was the last person he'd expected to see on his doorstep tonight. Her soft brown hair glistened under the light of the porch bulb. A pale blush warmed her cheeks and he had the urge to reach out and stroke her skin. He'd had the same urge when he'd stood over her in the yard. Even covered in mud, this woman had an unavoidable beauty.

"I wasn't sure if you were home."

"Sorry it took me so long to answer, I couldn't find my cane," he teased.

Allison's lips curved up into a smile and she raised her hand in a mock gesture of defeat. The corner of her smile pushed her round cheeks under her dark curled lashes. The affect stunned him. "All right, I deserve that. I was hoping we could start over. I come bearing gifts."

"Oh?" He leaned to the side and tried to look behind her back. "A present for me?"

"Well, indirectly, yes." From behind her back she produced a large plastic bottle filled with . . .

"Dog shampoo?"

"Sure. In case you hadn't noticed your dog is a mess."

With a dramatic hand placed over his heart, Will sighed. "I resemble that remark."

Allison laughed as she took in the sight of his muddied shirt and pants. "Yes, you certainly do."

Will took the bottle and stepped into the cluttered foyer. "I'm sorry about the mess, but Lizzie and I are just moving in." Suddenly self-conscious, Will wished he had cleaned up and paid a little closer attention to the house. Rolled carpets still lay up against the walls, and boxes sat everywhere. He glanced into the living room and swore under his breath for all the laundry stacked everywhere.

"Oh my. I didn't mean to intrude."

Will noticed the sudden change in temperature and wondered what had prompted it. "You're not intruding at all. We were just arguing about her wanting a new wardrobe. I think I was about to lose."

"Well, I'll just leave you two to hash it out. Tell your wife I'm sorry for bothering you so late."

Ahh. Suddenly, he realized what had caused the chill. She thought Lizzie was his wife. Although, why should she care? She was a stranger and surely she wasn't interested in him. Not that it mattered. He had two reasons for being in Brasselton; he had to supervise the renovation of this house–his and Lizzie's home–and build a new center. This town meant so much to Marty and she'd always dreamed of building here. Romance wasn't even a possibility.

"I don't think you understand." Will said, amused in spite of himself.

"Please don't explain. You don't have to tell me anything. It's none of my business."

"Why don't you come in and meet Lizzie before you go?" Will knew he should just tell her, but maybe this would cure her once and for all of making assumptions about people she didn't know.

"No, really. This isn't necessary." She tried to get back to the door, but tripped over a box that lay tipped over on the floor.

Will reached out and grabbed her arms to keep her from falling. Just when he thought he had her balanced, the carpet slid on the hardwood floor and both of them tumbled to the floor. He landed with a thud and she landed squarely on top of him.

"I'm sorry. I thought I had you." Will silently cursed the crack in his voice and shuddered from the wave of heat that rushed through him when she wiggled to get up. His mind told him to let her go, but his body made a damn fine argument about keeping her right where she lay. "Well, it seems as though I do."

"If you move your hands, I can get off."

He raised his eyebrow in amusement. "Oh?"

"You," she said quickly.

"Me, what?"

"You–off–I mean–"

Her face turned a blushing shade of pink and she let her head drop down to rest on his chest. He enjoyed the display.

"Oh, never mind."

"And just what exactly is going on in here?" Both of their heads snapped around when they heard the voice.

It was all he could do not to smile when Allison's face turned from rose petal pink to beet red. "Lizzie, honey this is Allison. She's one of our neighbors and she brought us a present."

"It's very nice to meet you, Allison," Lizzie said politely.

"Oomph!" Will struggled to catch his breath as Allison's knee dug mercilessly into his groin area. He jerked her up abruptly, in order to spare himself any more discomfort. After another jolt of pain shot through him, he wished he'd thought the action through more carefully.

"Oh my. I'm sorry. Did I hurt you?"

"Oh, no, I'm fine," he replied in a voice at least one octave higher than his usual. He scowled in Lizzie's general direction when he heard her giggle. "Could you gently remove your knee from my–"

After several minutes of cursing under her breath

and embarrassed glances toward Lizzie, Allison managed to get herself in an upright position. Will lay on the carpet watching her try to gain some semblance of composure. Lizzie leaned against the doorframe and eyed them both.

"I'm so sorry to have interrupted. I'll be going home now."

He almost let her go, but decided he wasn't quite finished staring at her shapely tanned legs. From his vantage point on the floor he had a wonderful view right up under her shorts to the hem of her white lacy panties.

"Lizzie, would you get our company some tea?"

"No, really," Allison protested.

"Go on, I'll take care of our guest." He laughed out loud as Lizzie reluctantly turned and left the room.

Will couldn't explain the amount of pleasure he gained from watching Allison squirm. Anyone else would have asked what he was doing with a wife who was obviously considerably younger than him, but not her. She just assumed.

"Are you going to get up or are you going to lie there all night?" She stood several feet away with her hands clasped in front of her. She looked as nervous as a cat on hot tin roof.

"Am I making you uncomfortable?"

"How can you be so nonchalant about this? Your wife just came in and found a strange woman lying on top of you and I'm supposed to act like nothing is wrong."

"It's okay, really." He slowly got up from the floor and brushed his khaki pants off. Not that it mattered. Hoyden had made a mess of his tan pants. He'd never be able to get them clean.

"How *can* it be?"

"Lizzie and I have a very open relationship. She has her life, I have mine, and I take care of her."

"What a chauvinistic attitude. I'd say it's pretty darn close to barbaric."

"My, you're just as full of opinions as you are assumptions." Will could see by the lines across her brow that he'd struck a nerve.

"This has nothing to do with me. It has to do with your obvious lack of respect for the female population. I can't imagine what she could possibly see in you."

"If you'd like I could give you some help with that one. I'd be more than glad to fill you in on some of my finer talents."

Her mouth dropped open so wide he could have driven a train into it. Her soft green eyes flashed with specks of anger, and he sensed her puckered pink painted lips were about to spit out some rather unpleasant words of advice for him.

"You are some piece of work. First your dog almost kills me–twice–then I end up humiliating myself in front of your wife and now you're actually coming on to me."

"I'm not coming on to you. I simply offered to give you some facts concerning particular skills I've acquired in my life." The more he said the more flustered she became. Her hands twitched in front of her and if he didn't know any better he'd swear her quivering knees were about to fail her. She was mad as hell and it looked good on her. "Besides, you and your car started it."

He mentally compared Allison to his last girlfriend, and wondered why he'd ever considered marrying Felicia. She'd been cold and lifeless. Although beautiful, she had no spirit or warmth.

"You're a feisty one, aren't you? I like that in my women."

"What you like or don't like in any woman is of no concern to me."

"No?"

"What's that suppose to mean?" She took a step away from him and he couldn't help but laugh. He moved forward and closed the distance between them.

Although he wasn't touching her, the warmth of her reached out to him. He raised one hand with the intention of convincing himself her skin was not as smooth as silk.

"What are you doing?" Her voice trembled when she spoke and its softness had a bizarre effect on his body.

"I'm not doing anything." *Yet.* He willed his heartbeat to slow to a normal rate and wished she would look away so he could wipe his sweaty palms on his pants legs.

He held his hand close to her cheek and imagined its smooth texture. He expected her to back away, or at least slap him, but she didn't move. He slowly tilted his head and leaned toward her. She turned her head just before his lips could cover hers. "This is so wrong," Allison whispered.

"How can it be?"

"Despite the fact that I find you somewhat attractive okay, very attractive, I refuse to let you do this to Lizzie."

"I told you, it's not what you think. In fact, I think Lizzie would be thrilled about the whole situation."

That one got him a good shove that sent him tripping over the bunched up carpet. For the second time in one night, he was flat on his back for no apparent good reason.

"You are sick!" She'd almost made it to the door when Lizzie burst through the swinging door carrying a tray of tea glasses.

"You're not leaving are you? I made mint tea. That's what took so long."

"Lizzie, I am so sorry. I didn't mean for–"

Will saw the confusion on Lizzie's face and knew his cover was about to be blown sky high.

"I'm sorry, Uncle Will. Did I take too long?"

◀ Three ▶

Allison stopped at the front door and turned around to look at Lizzie. Her facial expressions changed so quickly it amazed him. The only emotion he was sure he recognized was anger.

"*Uncle* Will?"

"Sure. My mom was his sister. I spent the last two years living with my aunt until a couple of weeks ago. Uncle Will let me come and live with him when my aunt got sick. He needs someone to take care of him."

Yeah, sick of not getting her hands on any more of your money, Will thought. He watched Allison's features soften and she released the doorknob. "Where are your parents? If you don't mind my asking."

Lizzie set the tray down on a nearby table and sat down in an overstuffed chair. Will's heart broke all over again at the sadness washing over her usually bright face.

"I'm sorry. Did I say something wrong?" Allison asked as she moved toward Lizzie.

Will pulled himself up off the floor and moved to stand behind Lizzie. He gently massaged her shoulders. "Marty, my sister, and her husband were killed in a car accident.

"I'm so sorry. I didn't know."

"It's okay. I just get sad sometimes and you kinda remind me of her."

Allison knelt down next to Lizzie and took her hand in her own. "I miss my mom, too. I came to town just before she died and I still haven't gotten used to her being gone."

"How long?" Lizzie asked wiping a tear off her cheek.

Will watched the way Lizzie warmed to Allison and experienced a twinge of jealousy. It passed quickly.

"Eight years in a couple of months."

Will noticed Allison looking at him and forced a smile to his face. "Lizzie and I haven't been together very long and it's a bit of an adjustment for both of us." This was hard on him, but not nearly as hard as it was on Lizzie. She needed a woman in her life. Allison and Lizzie becoming friends could be a good thing. For Lizzie, he told himself.

"I'm sure it is." Allison's voice sounded warm and sympathetic. Will thought he might be off the hook for his minor act of deceit, but his reprieve was short lived.

"Well, I really need to get going. Katie is at the house waiting for me."

"It was nice to meet you, Allison. I hope we can be friends."

"I'd like that, Lizzie."

Will had to hand it to Lizzie, she was a great kid.

Marty had done a great job raising her.

"It was nice of you to bring the present." Will tried to charm her with his most impressive smile, but she outdid him with her scowl.

"Oh yeah, what did she bring us?" Lizzie bounced out of the chair, again filling the role of an exuberant teenager.

"I brought pet shampoo. And as far as I can tell, you need it."

"Yeah, Hoyden's a mess all right." Will smiled.

"*Mm hmm*, her too," Allison offered.

Allison laughed, but Will knew the comment had been directed at him.

"Are you going to walk me out, Uncle Will?"

"What kind of gentleman would I be if I didn't?" He turned and winked at Lizzie before following his guest out the front door. "I'll be right back. I hope."

When he got outside, he found Allison standing with her arms folded across her chest and her foot tapping on the wooden porch.

"You should be ashamed of yourself," she barked.

"And why's that?" He folded his arms across his chest and tried to imitate her motions.

"You led me to believe Lizzie was your wife. I have never been so humiliated in my entire life."

"Never?" He knew he had her again. "Okay, so I got a little carried away, but I only did it to teach you a lesson."

"A little?" Allison asked.

"Besides, I never said we were married. In fact, I

said several times that it wasn't what you thought."

Allison looked at him expectantly. "What could you possibly hope to teach me from this whole mess?"

"Darlin', twice inside of two hours you've jumped to some pretty heavy assumptions about me. I would've thought you'd learned your lesson after the first time."

Her foot stopped tapping and one of her hands went up to cover her mouth. Will knew she was doing her best not to let him see her smile, but her green eyes sparkled with flecks of humor.

"Okay, you're right. I've learned my lesson."

Oh, I'm sure you have."

Allison puffed up with mock indignation. "Don't you be sarcastic with me. I said I'd learned my lesson."

"Are you sure? I'm available for private tutoring in that, as well as other areas, if you think you might need it."

"Oh, I'm sure you are. I think I'll be just fine."

"Okay, but if you change your mind, you know where to find me."

Her face glowed with the sincerity of her smile. The impact of it sent another wave of heat through him.

"It's late and I told Katie I wouldn't be long. I guess I'll see you around."

"Of that you can be sure."

Will watched Allison walk down the sidewalk and cross the street. He couldn't help remembering the view from underneath her. He wondered what other treasures he would find under her cotton shorts. He also wondered if he dared to find out. She had quite a temper and a woman like her would be quite a handful.

He wondered if he'd lost his mind. He'd all but mauled the poor woman in the hallway with Lizzie in the next room. He hadn't behaved so badly since high school and even then he wasn't that bad. Trouble was, he wasn't sorry. She'd set his insides to whirling and that hadn't happened in–well, never. Allison Ryder was some kind of woman and he had no intentions of staying away from her. He smacked his palm against his forehead. No romance, he reminded himself. "Oh brother."

He decided he'd think about it later. He went back in the house and sat down next to Lizzie on the sofa. She had her nose buried in a new romance novel she'd bought earlier in the day.

"So, what do you think, Liz?"

"Hmm, 'bout what?" she teased.

He snatched her book away.

"Hey, give that back, Uncle Will."

"Not until you tell me what you think."

"I think she's adorable, but she's not your type."

"What do you mean by not my type?" He should have seen the jibe coming, but thoughts of Allison's body pressed against his clouded his head. "How would you know what my type is? I don't even know."

"Mom always said you went straight for the brainless types. As far as I can see Allison doesn't come close to fitting into that category." Lizzie giggled when he poked her foot with the book he'd snatched.

"Well, everybody has off days. Maybe I can get lucky this time."

Will waited until Lizzie went up to bed before going back out to sit on the porch. He had a perfect view of Allison's house. He imagined her sitting in one of the wicker chairs with her feet propped up on the railing reading a book. He pictured himself sitting beside her. He looked up at the stars and the bright twinkling reminded him of the sparkle in her eyes.

Did she read? He wondered what kind of books. Would she enjoy sitting outside watching the stars? His heart skipped when he thought about Lizzie. Would it be fair to her to get into something with Allison? Too many questions and he wasn't sure he was ready for most of the answers.

"Katie, what do you think of my new neighbor?" Allison sat cross-legged on her living room floor. Katie sat across from her. On the floor between them sat several drained wine cooler bottles and an empty pizza box.

"I think he's probably one of the most handsome men I've ever seen."

"If you like that type." Allison tried to sound blasé, but she could tell by the grin on Katie's face that she hadn't pulled it off. "Oh stop looking at me like that."

"You like him, don't you?"

"How can you ask that, Katie? I only met him a few hours ago. Besides, he isn't the slightest bit interested in me." She remembered his teasing. "He's just a flirt."

Katie flung her hands into the air melodramatically. "How on earth did you reach that brilliant conclusion?"

"I could just tell." Allison stood up and gathered the mess from between them. When she walked into the kitchen she couldn't help looking out the window.

From her kitchen she had a clear view of Will's front porch. Her heart raced when she saw him sitting outside. She glanced up at the clock. How could it be midnight already? She stared across the street and wondered what he was doing. Was he thinking of her? Not likely. He wasn't going to think about her any more than she thought of him. She'd simply block him out of her mind and go on as if he didn't exist. She'd not give him a second thought.

"What's he doing?" Katie asked close to Allison's ear.

"Who?"

"Oh, don't give me that. He's been out there since you came back. I think he's watching you." Katie giggled and left the room.

"Oh, that's great, my own personal stalker." Allison stepped away from the window and turned the light off. Just to satisfy her own curiosity she stepped back to the window. He stood up and stared straight at her. Flustered, and not sure why, she stepped aside, but continued to stare out the window. Despite the distance, their gazes locked and she sensed for a brief moment that they shared the same thought. *Desire*.

Finally, he turned and went into the house. Allison left her kitchen and helped Katie straighten up the living room. Several minutes later, they took their respective places on the two sleeping bags they'd decided to use for the night.

"Katie?"

"Yeah."

"Do you really think he liked me?" Allison heard Katie chuckle softly.

"What do you care? You'll never do anything about it."

Allison bristled at her friend's statement. The saddest part was that Katie was probably right. However, she didn't have to be.

"Goodnight, Katie."

"'Night, Al."

Allison woke up from the worst night of sleep she'd ever had. From the moment she'd stepped away from Will's door, she'd not been able to get him out of her mind. She noticed Katie wasn't in her makeshift bed and wondered if she'd left. She stood and stretched the kinks out of her back. She was about to go upstairs when she heard voices in the kitchen. She walked to the kitchen door and pushed it open.

The last person she wanted to see in her kitchen at lord knows what time was Will Hoyt, but there he was, his deep brown eyes shining bright and clear. He shoved his fingers through his dark hair and the morning sun caught several streaks of gold. He looked too handsome.

Unable to gather her wits, she stood in the doorway, breathless.

"Good morning, sunshine." His gaze held hers and she couldn't look away. "We thought you were going to sleep the day away."

"What time is it?" Allison covered her mouth in an attempt to stifle a yawn. When she noticed Will's eyes drop to her legs, she realized that raising her arm had also raised the already short hem of her oversized T-shirt. She jerked her hand down and tugged at the bottom of her shirt.

"Allison, Will came over to invite us over for a barbecue this afternoon." Katie had already dressed in a peach floral summer dress.

How dare she look so good in my dress? She hated that Katie's perfect figure could pull off the look in a potato sack.

Allison looked down at her stained nightshirt and bare feet. She could only imagine what her hair must look like. "Great. What did you tell him?"

"Oh, I explained that I had to get home since Tony would be back by then, but I knew you didn't have any plans, so I assured him you'd love to join him and his niece."

Allison could tell by the way she emphasized the word niece, and by the twinkle in Will's eyes, that he'd told Katie what had happened the night before.

"Well, thanks so much for handling that for me."

"No problem, Sweetie." Katie smiled and gave her a wink.

"Did you two decide what time I was going over?" Allison asked. She really wanted to be angry with Katie, but couldn't muster up the will. She'd already decided, shortly before she finally fell asleep, that she was going to, at the very least, make friends with her new neighbors.

"Around noon is good for me," Will answered.

Allison looked at the clock and realized that if she was going to be at his house by noon she needed to get a few things done. She would have to squeeze a day's worth of chores into three hours. "Well then, I'd better get a move on."

Will stood to leave and she realized, for the first time, that he stood over six feet. She giggled aloud.

"What's so funny?" Will stared at her.

"I didn't realize how tall you are."

"And this is funny because?"

Without thinking Allison shot off her answer. "I guess it's the first time I've seen you totally vertical."

Katie covered her mouth and chuckled.

"I mean you didn't seem as tall when I was lying on top–"

"Allison," Katie whispered teasingly.

"I mean–oh never mind." The smile on his face addled her brain more than she liked to admit. What was it about this man that snapped her brain in half like a twig? Every time she was near him she became a bumbling idiot.

"Is tall a bad thing?" he asked, somewhat reluctantly.

"No, not at all," Allison answered.

"Well, I'm darn glad to hear that." He smiled, turned, and walked out the kitchen door. As he stepped off the porch, he called back, "See you at noon."

Allison plopped down in the kitchen chair and laughed.

"What is so funny?" Katie asked.

"You are. This is so obvious. I can't believe you're trying to play matchmaker at your age."

"What do you mean my age? I'm barely thirty." Katie pulled her shoulders back and lifted her chin indignantly.

"Yeah, and you're acting like a fourteen year old," Allison challenged.

"Well, chickie, if it were up to you, wedding bells would never ring."

"I'm not looking to get married. I'm doing just fine without a man in my life." Allison turned her head away so Katie couldn't see the lie in her eyes.

The truth was she was miserable without a man. She watched Katie and Tony together and envied their loving relationship. Then there was Justin; he had to be the sweetest little boy she'd ever met. Moreover, he never forgot to tell her how much he loved his Aunt Allie.

"Who are you trying to fool? I saw you all but

drooling over him."

"Who?" Allison felt the warmth rush into her cheeks.

"Don't give me who. Not that I blame you."

Allison stood and walked over to stand by the sink. She looked out the window and immediately her eyes turned to Will's front yard. She wasn't surprised to see him sitting on his front porch. She felt the blush in her cheeks flame when he waved at her.

"God, he's watching me," she breathed.

"Who?" Katie giggled. "I'd love to stay and watch you *not* drooling over the man you can't seem to take your eyes off, but haven't noticed. However, I need to get home so I can greet my men folk at the door when they come home with McDonald's fish sandwiches."

"Sure, abandon ship."

"You don't need me. Just let your instincts lead you. And for goodness sake wear something short and tight."

"I most certainly will not!" Allison stared wide-eyed at her best friend.

"Fine, die a lonely old spinster." Katie leaned forward, gave Allison a peck on the cheek, and left. "Love ya, girlfriend."

"Lord help me if you didn't." Allison smiled and blew a kiss across the room and watched the screen door slam shut. *Something short and tight, indeed.*

She sat holding her empty coffee cup for almost half an hour, trying to visualize everything in her closet. *Do I even own anything short and tight?* There was only one way to find out.

Twenty minutes later, she stood in front of her closet door wearing nothing but a towel. She looked in the full-length mirror before opening the door. Well she owned one thing that would suit Katie's description, but she sure as heck wasn't going over to Will's house in a towel.

She started with a bright pink floral summer dress that made her face look pale. It ended up in a heap on her closet floor. The short blue plaid skirt and navy tank top wouldn't do with Hoyden anywhere around. She tossed the tank over onto the bed and the skirt dropped to the floor.

She finally settled on a pair of emerald green shorts and a black V-neck T-shirt. She stood in front of the mirror trying different hairstyles. First up, then to one side, finally she pulled it back in a banana clip that matched her shorts.

She stood in front of the mirror and stared at her reflection. The shorts were well above her knees and the shirt hugged her snugly. "Even this would do Katie proud," she mumbled aloud.

After she gathered up the two-liter bottle of soda she'd found in the pantry, she headed out the back door. On the way across the street, it occurred to her she hadn't gotten anything accomplished all morning.

Will met her at the curb and took the bottle of soda. "Thanks, but you didn't need to bring anything."

Allison smiled. "I know, but not everyone shares my preference of soda and I can be kinda grumpy when I don't get my own way."

"Really? I hadn't noticed." Will's eyes lit up with a mischievous sparkle.

Allison stepped around the pile of dog toys in the back yard and looked around for Hoyden. "Where's the baby?"

"I locked her inside to save you what's left of your dignity." She sensed Will's embarrassment at the previous day's entanglements and felt bad for how she'd behaved.

"Really, that's not necessary. I love animals."

His eyebrows shot up. "I guess I just figured–"

"You assumed?"

"Okay, I assumed you didn't like animals, or at least dogs. You were pretty angry."

"In my line of work I don't have much of a choice. Even so, I love animals, especially dogs." She followed Will across the yard. "I was just caught off guard, is all."

"What do you do?" Will opened a lawn chair and sat it next to her.

Allison noticed he didn't sit down himself until after she did. *A gentleman, nice.* "I work at Katie's Care Shelter and Salon."

His expression changed and she wondered if she'd misunderstood his question. Then he smiled and she relaxed again.

"Do you like it? I mean working there?"

"Oh, I love it. We have some of the cutest animals and some of them have been there for years. The animals are just about the sweetest things."

"Why don't you adopt them out? I mean, it must be expensive to keep them."

"They're all misfits. Right now we don't have too many. Maybe a half dozen dogs, a couple of cats, and a few others."

"You and Doc take care of them alone, or do you have other employees?"

Allison turned toward him. Most people, even those who lived in town didn't know Doc, he was somewhat of a recluse. "How do you know Doc?" She waited, but he didn't answer right away.

"We've met on one or two occasions. Nice guy."

"Yes, he is. I'm gonna miss him." Allison tried not to dwell on her impending unemployment, but she hated the thought of all those animals being moved to a different facility and being destroyed. Not everyone shared her ideas on strays and misfits. No animal should be put down because he wasn't perfect.

"Tell me about your animals." He stood up and moved over next to the grill.

Allison watched him move around preparing the coals and setting up the dishes on the table. All of a sudden he appeared tense and a bit nervous. He listened while he worked.

"We have a raccoon named Tippy and she's the sweetest thing in the world."

"Why's her name Tippy?" Will set the steaks across the metal rack and sprinkled seasoning over them.

Allison could already smell the juices dripping onto the hot coals. She watched him bend over to close the bag of charcoal. The way his shorts pulled across his rear end and the muscles in his thighs tightened, took her breath away. She warmed when he turned around and caught her staring.

"Allison?"

When she finally tore her gaze away from his lower body, she made it as far as his chest. The navy blue pullover fit tight enough to accentuate the ripple of his stomach and the sleeves hugged the muscles in his arms. What a lucky shirt.

"Allison?" he asked her again.

"Very lucky," she mumbled.

"Who's lucky? Where are you?" He stood in front of her with his hands on his hips.

She jerked her head around so he couldn't see her face. "Nothing." God, why does this always happen to me?

"Allison, are you going to tell me about Tippy?"

"She's a leg with three raccoons." Looking at him rattled her like a trailer in a Texas tornado.

"How exactly does something like that happen?"

Allison faced him and stared. "It was an accident."

"Obviously." Will laughed and the sound of his genuine humor warned her something was amiss. "Must have been a hell of an accident to leave a leg with three raccoons."

"What are you talking about?" Somewhere in the course of their conversation she'd got lost. She played back the words in her mind. "Oh my."

"Ah, I hear the bells," Will teased.

"I'm sorry, my mind was on something else."
Yeah, your butt.

Will had turned and focused his attention on tending to the steaks, when Allison got it from behind. The all too familiar warmth of Hoyden's tongue slithering up the back of her neck sent a chill along the length of her spine.

"Hold still, Allison. You have a giant hairy pest on your neck." Will lunged in her direction wielding the spatula. Neither she, nor the dog flinched. For some unexplainable reason Allison trusted Will not to hurt her.

Allison turned around to find soft brown eyes staring into hers. "Hi ya, girl." Hoyden nuzzled up to her neck and she smiled. The tip of the pup's tongue slid in and out, bathing Allison with sloppy puppy kisses.

"I can't believe how she's taken to you."

Will kneeled down next to her and the dog. He rested his hand on her knee to steady himself. He was so close she could smell his woodsy aftershave and the lingering smell of hickory smoke. She closed her eyes and inhaled deeply. She could think of a few things to do with him in the woods.

"She loves having her neck rubbed," Will offered, gently massaging the fur on Hoyden's neck. The retriever's head lolled sideways and her tongue dangled out the side of her mouth.

"So I see. She also loves to neck." Allison reached back and wiped some of the excess slobber off her neck. "I believe this belongs to you," she said as she wiped her hand on his sleeve. The feel of his muscle tightening under her hand made her stop. She stared at his shoulder and knew she should pull her hand away, but she couldn't.

"You must–work out," she stammered.

"I get my exercise. I actually hate working out so I'm trying to find more interesting ways to get my exercise."

His gaze locked with hers. She would've had to be blind not to see the smoldering desire there. "Have you found any?" Allison couldn't pull her gaze away and she didn't want the moment to end, not just yet.

"I have a few ideas. I guess maybe I could share them with you. Are you up for the challenge?"

"I think I can handle it." Allison wasn't sure, but she thought maybe the temperature had just gone up a good ten degrees in a matter of seconds. Sweat beaded on the back of her neck and her palms grew slick.

"I'll bet you can." Will leaned toward her.

His breath blew softly across her lips. She felt his hand slide up on her thigh and her own breath caught. Another ten degrees.

"Hey, Allison. What's up?" Lizzie's chipper voice broke the silence and the mood.

"I am," Will mumbled under his breath. Allison waited for him to move; he hesitated, but finally pulled his hand away.

"Hi, Lizzie. Thanks for inviting me over. I was wondering what to do with my weekend off."

"Actually, it was all Uncle Will's idea to invite you. He talked about you all last night. I hardly got any sleep."

Allison looked at Will and laughed when she saw the grill fork pointed at his throat and his tongue hanging out to the side of his mouth. Had he really been talking about her?

"Well, thank you for sharing that with us all, Lizzie. Now go pack your stuff, I'm sending you back to the orphanage."

Amused by his theatrics, Allison giggled. "It doesn't matter who came up with the idea. I'm just glad to be here," she said, leaning back in her lawn chair and propping her feet up on the seat of Will's vacated chair. "So what do you do, Will?"

For a brief moment his face registered a look resembling alarm. Then he smiled. "I build things."

"What kind of things?" Allison sensed his reluctance to answer her question and decided to pursue the issue a little bit further. "Buildings? Boats? What?"

"Fitness centers." He stood facing the grill and Allison wondered why he wouldn't look at her.

"So, you'll be commuting back and forth from the city?" She stood up and walked toward him.

"No." Will turned around and handed her a plate with a perfectly cooked steak on it.

"Are you retiring or something? I can't imagine

there would be much work for you here in Brasselton." Allison had almost made it back to her chair when he responded.

"You'd be amazed." He took a step closer and his expression became serious. "I specialize in small communities. It was Marty's way of helping real people. It's hard to understand."

"Understand what?"

"I inherited Marty's business when she–died." She was so heavy as a child and nothing seemed to work for her."

"How sad," Allison said softly.

"Well, she got a job so she could join a fitness club and with the exercise and a diet her doctor put her on, she changed her entire life."

"What a wonderful story. It's hard for some people to make that commitment."

Will sat on the picnic table bench. "Well, she was so inspired that she went to college and learned about nutrition and architecture." Will smiled. "Yeah, unique combination. She spent most of her adult life building a distinctive line of fitness centers in small towns."

Allison leaned forward in her chair and looked at him intently. "I wouldn't think there would be much money in that. Although, small towns are so laid back I could see the need."

Will got up and pulled his own steak off the grill and rejoined her at the table. "That's what makes them so exceptional. They're owned by a small group of people who also understand the importance of health, especially in farming communities. The memberships are low cost so the number of members is higher and it evens out. People can afford to go and get the help they need to stay fit and healthier."

"That's wonderful!"

Her enthusiasm touched him and made what he needed to tell her even harder. "I didn't have any idea who you were or what you did when I made this deal. I just don't want you to think you had anything to do with it or that it had anything to do with you. Or even that this has anything to do with it or you."

"You're rambling, Will."

"I am?"

"What are you talking about?" Allison stood, staring at him. She could tell by the expression on his face, his news wasn't good. She couldn't imagine he'd had enough time to feel the need to tell her that she was a nice girl and he just wanted to be friends.

She picked up her plate and moved toward the potato salad.

◄ Four ►

"Allison, I'm the company that bought the property from Doc."

The plate slipped from her hands and they both reached at the same time to catch it. She hadn't expected that. "What are you saying?"

"Now, hear me out. I had no idea you worked at the shelter when I bought the property. I didn't know. I swear."

"Would it have made any difference?" Allison's hands shook and she needed to hit something. He was the reason she was going to be unemployed. All those poor little animals were going to be homeless or worse–put down.

"Well, no, but–"

Allison spun around and headed out of the backyard. How could she explain to him what he was doing? Worse yet, how could she explain why it mattered so much to her? She looked up at the house where she saw Lizzie staring out the screen door. His hand on her arm stopped her.

"Listen to me. Maybe we can find another place for you to move the shelter to."

"What good would that do? Even if we could

afford it. You don't get it do you?"

"Get what?" Will asked.

He looked genuinely concerned, but she couldn't let that sway her. She needed to be angry with him. More than that, she wanted to be angry with him. If she could hold on to those emotions perhaps it would lessen the effects of the physical attraction she felt toward him.

"That's the only home they have. The land is theirs. It's what they know. They can roam as they please and they're familiar with it." Acres of open spaces specifically landscaped for their safety and protection had been carefully maintained. No, nothing else would work. Allison tried to walk away, but he stopped her again.

"Al, wait."

She turned on him. "Don't call me that! Only my friends call me that."

"Why can't we be friends?"

Tears welled in her eyes and Allison looked at him with no pride. Her mother would have accused her of being melodramatic, but she couldn't help it. Hell, she cried at long distance commercials, and she'd still never seen *Bambi* or the *Lion King* without bawling her eyes out.

"I know you may not understand this, but those animals are a lot like me. They're all alone. They don't have anyone to take care of them, except me. And I have them."

"You don't have to be alone and I said I would

help you find new homes for them. How many animals are there?"

"You can't be serious. This isn't some poor little charity event you can make brownie points at."

"I'm serious. How hard can it be to find homes for a few dogs and cats? Unless you don't want my help." The challenge had been issued and she was going to call him on it.

After hearing him talk about his sister's dreams and all she'd been through, he should be able to understand the importance of these animals' survival. She quietly contemplated how to handle the situation. It would do little good to alienate him. She'd never gain his support if she did that. Finally, something occurred to her.

"Okay, Mr. Compassionate, but you have to do it my way. Deal?" If he had a personal investment perhaps it would make a difference. Once he spent time at the shelter he would see the consequence of losing it.

A deep crease appeared across his forehead and she was certain he was about to call it quits, before they'd even got started.

"What are the terms?" Will folded his arms across his chest and stared her down.

His eyes sparkled with the excitement of a challenge and she was again struck by the intensity of his good looks. "You have to spend the next week getting to know the animals."

She laughed when his shoulders slumped slightly.

"Why? How?"

"Fine. Never mind."

"Wait a minute, I just asked why."

Allison took a step closer to him and the heat from his body radiated through her clothes. *Tactical error. No fraternizing with the enemy.* "You can't really expect to find good homes for animals you know nothing about. Can you?"

"Uh, no." Will looked away sheepishly, avoiding eye contact. "I guess not."

"Good, we'll start first thing in the morning. Unless you have other plans." Allison gave him one last opportunity to back out, but he stood firm.

"I'm all yours."

Allison could barely stand the heat. Even with the inches between them, she could feel him without actually touching him. He reached up and hooked her chin with his finger.

"Allison, I'm really sorry."

"We'll see." Allison knew she was being stubborn, but she had to be strong for the animals, as well as herself. She let Will convince her to stay for dinner and the remainder of the afternoon went without incident. They sat in the yard talking about what they liked to do in their spare time. Will told her about some of the places he'd visited and she was eager to hear as much about his life as he was willing to share. Once she put him through the wringer at the shelter, he'd probably never speak to her again. She'd take whatever time she could get.

His eyes sparkled with enthusiasm as he spoke of some of his own projects in more exotic locales. She noticed that when he spoke of his visits home he smiled. A small dimple creased his cheek and offered a glimpse at a boyish charm hidden somewhere beneath the surface. He looked like a man, and he talked about business like a man, but she saw something more.

"I never imagined I would ever find myself living in Texas. Much less a town the size of a pea." He laughed. "I guess someone forgot to tell these folks that everything in Texas is big."

"Well, you fit right in." Will lay on the bench of the picnic table and Allison thought, for being a city boy he did look pretty at home in the country surroundings.

"Don't get me wrong, I like it here."

"But?" Allison tilted her head and waited for his response.

"I just can't figure out what I'm supposed to do with my spare time. I doubt if Brasselton has much of a night life."

Allison smiled. "You'd be amazed at how much there is to do at night around here."

He turned to her and his eyebrow lifted. "I can hardly wait to find out for myself."

Embarrassed by her own suggestive remarks, she stood. "I think it's time for me to go home."

Will got up and came to stand next to her. "Won't you stay and watch the sun go down with me?"

"I don't want to intrude on your time with Lizzie.

She's been inside almost all day."

Will barked out a laugh. "Are you kidding? She has a mountain of books in there to read. We may not see her for days."

"Are you sure?" Allison didn't really want to leave; despite his news about Doc's land, she enjoyed being with him.

"You'd be saving me from an evening of watching the cover of her book bob as she reads." Will took her hand in his and fluttered his eyelashes at her. "Besides, I haven't actually watched a Texas sunset and I'd hate to see my first one alone."

Allison couldn't help being tempted by his persuasiveness. "Well, if it would mean that much to you." She lowered her lashes.

When she looked up at him again, his grin ripped her senses to shreds. He had a smile that did things to her she wasn't aware could happen.

"I know just the spot to watch from."

Allison followed him to the side of the house and stopped next to a doublewide hammock. She stood staring at the mesh contraption and her knees went weak. She closed her eyes and her mind conjured a mental picture of the two of them laying in it.

Will knew he was pushing his luck, but something inside him said he would come out on top. He nearly groaned aloud at the thought. "Word has it, my grandpa, Wilfred, used this very hammock to court my grandmother."

Her cheeks turned a soft shade of pink and he

liked knowing they had already begun making memories.

"And you expect it to still hold us?"

"If we're lucky." Will nudged her toward the hammock, half expecting her to refuse, but to his surprise she didn't. He watched her swing it back and forth a few times. She tugged on the hooks holding it between the two trees. She even stretched a few spots of the weave.

"Are you going to sit in it, or inspect it?" He couldn't help laughing. From her expression, you'd think he'd just offered her a death trap.

Allison held her hand out and offered him first crack at the hammock. "You first."

"If I get in, you have to come too." He swallowed the sudden lump in his throat and grinned at her.

"If it holds you, I'll be more than glad to join you."

Will gently lowered himself onto the hammock. He bounced around a few times testing the weight and hoped it would hold. He held out his hand to Allison and waited for her to join him. He'd sat across from her all day long wishing he could figure out how to get close to her. Ever since he'd told her about buying the property, she'd been cool at best. She'd listened to him talk about life in Beverly Hills and the high rises in New York City. She'd even seemed interested in some of it, but she'd kept her distance.

"Come on, I won't bite." *Unless you ask me to.*

When she took his hand, the warmth of her skin washed over every inch of his body. She positioned herself next to him and waited to see if the strings would hold them both.

"Well, it seems okay."

He rolled a little to the side and watched her swing her legs up. Her silky smooth calves rubbed against his, sending his hormones into an immediate state of chaos. Even the dark hair covering his legs didn't veil the sensual glide of flesh on flesh.

"Just relax. What's the worst thing that could happen?" He paused. "Okay, never mind. Let's just enjoy the view."

"I can do that."

Allison lay back and hesitated when her shoulder made contact with his arm. He hadn't meant to put his arm around her, but the hammock didn't allow much room for positioning. After a few seconds, she settled back and her muscles relaxed.

The sky started to fade into a kaleidoscope of vivid colors before they'd settled in. For the first time in months, he laid back and the stress of his everyday life and everything he'd gone through slipped away. He had a beautiful woman lying in his arms watching a masterpiece in progress. Never in his life could he ever have imagined there were so many shades of orange or red.

He remained speechless as the cornflower blue sky turned into a blaze of red and amber before fading into splashes of coral with touches of honey. He'd never thought any of these colors actually existed, until now. The burnished horizon set off the golden color of

Allison's legs. Somewhere in the span of a second, the sky disappeared and all he could see was her.

His neighbor burned against him and he needed to do something to cool off or he'd surely burst into flames. He'd been with more than enough women and not one of them could claim to have had this kind of effect on him.

"I've never seen anything like it my life," Will whispered. He stared down at the top of her head.

She nodded.

"I make a point of watching the sun set at least once a week. It helps keep me in touch with what's important."

"What is important to you, Al?" He waited for her to correct him about the nickname, but she said nothing. "Money?"

"Lord, no. Money doesn't even rank in the top ten. I've never had much, so I don't miss it."

"I've never gone without so I guess I find that hard to understand."

Allison shifted until she lay facing him and pressed her hand against his chest to balance herself. When he opened his eyes, she was staring at him.

"Are you okay, Will? Do you want me to get up?"

Her lips moved, but he couldn't hear her. All he heard was the world rushing by and his heart beating. Was it his heart? He could feel the softness of her breast pushing against him and he could feel every breath she took. He knew it had to be her breath. He'd stopped breathing the second her body had touched his.

"Will? What's wrong?" The concern in her voice snapped him out of his trance.

"What would you do if I kissed you?" The words slipped out before he could decide if he should say them.

Her auburn brows went up and her eyes grew wider, but she didn't move. He wanted to kiss her so badly it scared him.

"I don't know."

"Well, I don't think I can stop myself, so if you're gonna hurt me, tell me now so I can brace myself."

When she didn't say anything, he lowered his head until his lips brushed hers.

"Will," she whispered.

"Too late." He took her mouth in a way he didn't think was possible. It started slow and careful, but he couldn't stop there. She sighed against him and he snapped.

He pulled the clip loose and let the soft strands of her hair fall around his fingers. He wrapped it around his fingers and pulled her closer.

Her hands pushed against him. Did she want him to stop? No, his mind argued. She's on top. He realized she was working her way up his body.

"Will?" She whispered against his mouth and he started to pull away. She grabbed his face and pulled him back into the kiss.

Her leg wrapped around his and her hands ruffled through his hair. Her lips tasted like some kind of exotic fruit. Sweet and tender. Every nerve in his body vibrated with the intensity of her response and he told himself to stop. Too bad his body ignored his mind. His hand found its mark and his palm filled with the softness of her curved bottom.

Carefully, he pulled her farther on top of him. The hammock swung and they both stilled to let it settle.

"Uncle Will? Telephone."

Will opened his eyes and before he could stop her Allison tried to bolt up.

"No, Al!"

The hammock swung once and with no more warning than that, it dropped them both into a massive pile of tangled arms and legs under the swinging contraption.

Will could tell by the look Allison gave him it would be best to hold his tongue, but when had he ever heeded a warning with anything less than rebellion? "I'd say this would be the worst. What do you say, Al?"

"I–you–oh–"

Will lie on the ground and watched her scurry up and out of his yard. If he didn't know better, he'd have sworn she was glowing in the dark.

It took some time for him to regain his bearings. The impact of their intimacy had left him reeling. It had also brought up a lot of doubts and questions. It was entirely too soon to have to worry about having feelings for her, but he did.

Several hours later, he lay in bed, tossing and turning, trying to get her out of his mind, and failing miserably. Sleep came much later.

* * *

"What's all the racket out there?" Will pulled the sheet off the bed and wrapped it around his naked body. He stepped over Hoyden who lay next to his bed.

"Uncle Will, there's a truck out front and whoever it is keeps honking the horn."

Will met Lizzie in the dark hallway and they stared at each other, bleary-eyed. "Well, they'll go away if we ignore them." They turned around to go back to their rooms and the horn blared again. "Geez!"

Will decided he'd had enough and stomped down the stairs. The front door banged the wall when he flung it open. He stalked down the front walkway. Twice he had to stop and pull the sheet back around him. When he reached the pickup truck, he tapped on the darkly tinted window.

He heard the buzz of the electric window as it rolled down.

"Good morning, sunshine." Allison sat behind the wheel grinning out at him.

"What the hell are you doing here, Allison? It's still dark outside." Will turned around and headed toward the house. "Go back to bed."

Allison turned off the engine and hopped out of the truck. "No way. We have to be to work in thirty minutes."

Will stopped and regarded her seriously. "No, we don't. *We* are our own boss and *we* sleep in. Goodbye, Allison." Again, he started walking.

"Fine. Then I'll tell Doc the animals can keep their home."

Will wasn't a morning person to begin with and something about being threatened just wasn't setting right. "Look you, pseudo-perky little thing."

"No! You look. I made you an offer and you accepted that offer. I would think as a business man you'd be honorable enough to follow through on a deal."

"Allison, what time is it?"

She stood with her arms folded over her chest and her foot tapping on the concrete. "Does it matter?"

Will took a step toward her and stopped. "If it's before seven, you'd better be prepared for the consequences." He took another step. He reached out and grabbed her wrist. She tried to pull away.

"Stop it, Will. What are you doing?"

"Your watch. Show me your watch."

She stopped pulling and turned her wrist for him to see. "Allison," he tried to keep his voice even and calm, "it's only five o'clock in the stinkin' morning."

"I know, but the animals are hungry and they need to be fed." She took a step away from him.

Allison's wide-eyed expression told him he had her on the run and he liked it. "Well, since you chose to take the risk, you need to know there is only one reason I am willing to be awake at this hour."

She took another step back and slowly lowered her arms to her side. She looked like she was about to bolt, but he wasn't going to let her get away.

"Wh–what's that?" she asked.

"Funny you should ask." Without warning he reached out and snaked his arm around her waist. "It ain't coffee. He lowered his head and covered her mouth with his before she could protest.

Her lips softened, but she'd decided not to part them for him. Hell, he thought, as long as I'm up I might as well make the effort.

He pulled back far enough to look at her face. "I'm gonna win." He took her mouth again, but this time he was determined to taste her fully. He had one hand in the small of her back pulling her as close against him as possible. He put his other hand on the back of her neck and slowly massaged. After several seconds, her defenses went down and she melted against him. Her lips parted and his legs went weak when his tongue met hers. His hands were on her and God help him–her hands were on him. Her fingertips trailed down the length of his back. Good thing he had the sheet or she'd be meeting up with–

"Oh my," Allison rasped against his lips. "You're naked."

"No I'm not." Then all of a sudden he had the strangest feeling she might be right. He pulled his hand out of her hair and reached down for the sheet he was sure he'd wrapped around him. He realized the only thing between him and total nudity was her. The sheet hung dangerously close to falling to the ground. If it weren't for her standing up against him it would have.

"You didn't even get dressed before you came out

here?"

Will pulled the sheet up around him and stepped back. "Guess I'd better get dressed, huh?"

"Yeah," she stammered, breathless. "We have to get going."

Will looked down at her, planted a quick kiss on her mouth, and walked away. "You can make coffee while I find some clothes."

"You said you didn't–"

"I lied." When Will looked back at her she was standing in the same spot he'd left. "I'm not going without coffee. So you better get a move on." He left the door open.

He took his time going upstairs to pull on his jeans when he smelled the aroma of fresh coffee brewing. He smiled at his reflection in the mirror. "I always win."

By the time Will came downstairs, Allison had already gone back out to the truck. He walked toward her like he didn't have a care in the world. He looked fully awake and refreshed in his blue jeans and T-shirt. In fact, he looked incredible. Allison jerked her head around when he caught her staring at him.

Again.

"Sorry it took so long. I had some trouble finding my shoes." He took the cup of coffee she handed him.

Allison nodded and started the truck's engine. "Fine."

"Look, Al. About what happened a few minutes ago . . . ."

"Forget it. It's not a big deal." She thought he looked hurt, but couldn't tell for sure in the dark.

"Really?" His voice was rough and she could tell he was irritated. What she didn't know was why.

"I should have called to wake you up before I came over." Allison kept her gaze focused on the road. She tried to ignore the heat burning her up. God, are the windows fogging up?

They sat quietly for several minutes, neither of them having anything to say. Finally, he broke the silence. "So, what exactly is it you do all day long? I mean how hard can it be to take care of a few little animals?

"How hard? Well, I reckon in about half an hour you'll know for yourself."

"Don't get defensive. I've never had a pet before Hoyden. I like animals and all, but never really had time to take care of one."

Allison turned her head and looked at him. "If you've never had a pet, what made you get a dog like Hoyden?"

"I didn't get her."

"I'm confused."

Will smiled but made no comments. "She was a prearranged gift for Marty. Her husband had bought and paid for the pup before it was born, as a gift."

"Oh, that's so sweet. But I thought–"

"Yeah. Hoyden came along about eight months ago and Lizzie wanted her. Grace said no, but I fought her on principle."

"What principle would that be?" Allison kept her eyes pointed straight ahead but listened carefully.

"The dog was a love gift between Lizzie's mom and dad. I loved Marty and she would have wanted Lizzie to have the pup. Plus Grace hated dogs and it really bugged her."

The sun slowly peeked up and the street lamps gave her enough light to see the wicked grin on his face. He was handsome as the devil and she figured he didn't even know it. At twenty-seven years old, she'd only dated four men. All but one of them had been hometown boys who weren't gonna win any beauty contests. Mitchell had been different. He had the body of a Greek statue and a face born to be in pictures. His biggest problem had been letting anyone forget how handsome he was. He had no personality and no sense of humor. Will had boatloads of both.

"So, why don't you and Grace get along? If you don't mind me asking." Allison feared she'd stepped onto forbidden ground, but took another step anyway. "Lizzie seems to like her."

"Yeah, well, Lizzie doesn't know all the facts."

She sensed a change in his mood and wished she hadn't asked. "We don't have to talk about this. I'm sorry." Allison looked over at him. He sat facing straight ahead, his hands clenched into fists.

"Grace didn't do it, but she's the reason Marty is dead."

◀ Five ▶

Allison heard the agonizing pain in his voice and wanted to reach out to him. She kept her gaze on the road. She had to watch for the turn-off to the shelter.

"Marty loved working in the business. It was the only thing that could drag her away from Coop and Lizzie."

"Coop was her husband?" Allison asked softly.

"Yeah. He was a great guy. Everyone liked him from the start. He swept Marty off her feet and they were married within a month of meeting. She always said Coop was her destiny."

"How did they meet?"

"He came into the office looking for a contractor. At first he refused to deal with a woman and she felt sorry for him because he couldn't see past the end of his nose." Will laughed. "She decided on the spot to teach him a lesson and make him not only acknowledge her talent as a good contractor, but fall in love with her to boot."

Allison turned the truck onto the dirt road. Will didn't comment on the roughness of the drive.

"Grace thought Marty was beneath him and did everything in her power to get Coop to drop Marty.

When they got married she never accepted my sister into her family."

"How horrible for Marty."

"Oh no. Don't feel sorry for Marty. She made Grace's life a living hell. She went out of her way to get Coop to take her over there every chance she got. She would call and tell me about some family gathering where the entire family would sit around doting on her and Grace would just eat."

Allison smiled. "Sounds like Marty had lots of spunk. Actually, she sounds a lot like you." Pulling the truck up under a tree, Allison turned off the engine, but neither of them got out.

Will smiled and unshed tears glistened in his eyes. "We were the best of friends and she understood me like no one else."

"I've always wished I'd had a brother or sister. But I'm an only child."

"All hell broke loose when Marty got pregnant with Lizzie. They changed their wills, so in the event of death, Lizzie would get everything and a trustee would be appointed."

"Was Grace to be the trustee?"

"Not even close. I was. Grace saw the will and it infuriated her. It took some time, but it finally died down. Lizzie was the light of both her parent's eyes. I've never seen two prouder people."

"I assume Grace loved Lizzie since she took her in after the death."

"I guess in her own twisted way she did. The

thought of not getting her hands on the estate ate away at her. She constantly made remarks about Marty making Coop blind to his real family. What gets me is, the business was Marty's before she ever met Coop."

"So, I still don't understand how their deaths were Grace's fault." Allison pulled into her parking spot and turned the engine off. Will didn't move. She sat and waited for him to finish.

"Coop was due to get back from a business trip and Marty had a problem at one of the sites she had a crew at. Grace couldn't be bothered with babysitting so Marty took Lizzie with her." Will let his head lean back against the truck window. "Grace showed up at the site and Lizzie was with one of the employees. Marty wouldn't have left Lizzie with anyone she didn't trust."

"Of course she wouldn't," Allison consoled.

"Grace marched in and said she was there to pick up Lizzie, who verified that her mom had tried to call and that Grace was in fact her aunt. Grace took her off without even telling Marty."

"What right did she have?"

Will banged his fist against the door and Allison jumped. "That's just it. She had no right. By the time Coop got to Marty, a storm front had moved in. He calmed her down and then they took off to make the twenty minute drive to get Lizzie."

He stopped and she thought she saw tears falling, but he looked away.

"Coop was a great driver, but the drunk guy

coming toward them wasn't."

Allison covered her mouth with her hand. She struggled to swallow around the lump in her throat and willed herself not to cry. She could hear his heart breaking with each crack in his voice.

"Coop was thrown from the car and died instantly. Marty wasn't so lucky. She was trapped in the passenger seat for over an hour, only alive enough to suffer. She struggled to stay awake while they tried to cut her out."

"Will, you don't have to tell me this. It's none of my business." Allison moved to climb out of the truck. Will's hand on hers stopped her. He twined his fingers with hers and held on.

"No, I need to tell someone. I've never talked about it and I need to."

Allison squeezed his hand. "Okay."

"The medics said Marty stayed semi-coherent through the entire ordeal and stayed that way until she got to the hospital. They said that over fifty percent of her body was crushed."

"Couldn't they have saved her? I mean, with all of modern science there must have been something they could do." Allison's eyes filled with tears. Her chest tightened at the thought of feeling life slip away and not being able to do anything.

"Grace made it to the hospital just before Marty died. She refused to let Lizzie go in to see her mother. What she did do was scream at Marty that she'd killed Coop with her stupid construction business."

"How could that be?" Allison whispered. "What kind of woman would do that?"

"Grace told her she should have been home trying to be a real mother instead of doing God knows what. The nurse at the hospital had to drag Grace out of the room."

"Good for the nurse."

"It didn't matter. The last thing Marty heard in this world was Grace calling her a murderer and telling her that her daughter would be better off without a mother like her."

"Oh, Will, I can't imagine Marty would believe that. She had to know she was a wonderful mother. That had to be a comfort for her as she passed on. I feel it as sure as I feel you." She squeezed his hand again and he smiled at her.

"I know you're right. Lizzie is an outstanding kid and it's because of Marty and Coop. No one else."

Guilt stabbed at Allison at having opened the subject and needed to make amends for his memories being stirred. "You know we don't have to do this today. We can put it off until you're feeling better."

Will pulled her hand up to his lips and brushed them across her knuckles. "This won't ever go away, and as you so kindly reminded me earlier, a deal is a deal."

"Are you sure?"

"I'll bet those critters are getting hungry." Will let go of her hand and they climbed out of the truck.

Allison locked the doors and led him into the

building. Chatters and soft growls welcomed them, bringing a smile to Allison's lips.

"Al, this is great." Will walked around the room. "What's that table for?"

"That's where you'll clip toe nails."

"Whose nails am I going to clip?" Will picked up the peculiar looking clippers and snapped the handle several times. "Seems to me like the little fellas wouldn't like that much."

Allison laughed. "They adjust quickly." She moved around the table and headed for a door.

"Where we going now?" Will followed along behind her.

"I think it's time you meet my little friends. You have to make sure you give them a chance to get used to your scent before you get too close."

"Geez, you make them sound dangerous."

"Well, if they think *they're* in danger, they can be. You have to remember, we don't have just dogs and cats."

"Oh, that's right, you have a three raccooned leg." Will wasn't sure if she remembered her slip. Her lips curled up into a bright smile and he knew she did.

"A gentleman wouldn't bring up something like that to a lady."

Will moved closer and leaned down toward her face. "Who said I was a gentleman?" He smiled when her breath caught. He reached up and wrapped a lock of her soft brown hair around his finger.

Gently, he pulled her face closer, until her breath

brushed across his mouth. He shifted his weight from one leg to the other, hoping to ease some of the tension in his jeans.

"Are you here to work or play, Will?"

"That depends on the boss."

"Well, the boss says this is a hands on job."

"That's my favorite kind." Will lifted his hand and put it on the back of her neck. The further she let him go, the hotter he got. She smelled like a fresh flower garden and it was driving him crazy. He looked down into her sparkling eyes.

Did she have any idea what it did to him when she slid her tongue across her bottom lip like that? She moved her arms and he waited to feel them slip around him.

When she spoke, her voice was soft and seductive. "Then you won't mind carrying that bag of dog food into the back room for me. Right?" She laughed and gently shoved him away from her.

Will let out the breath he'd been holding. "Sure, boss."

Allison stepped away from him and if he hadn't seen the sweat on her upper lip, he'd think she was immune to him.

He slung the bag over his shoulder and followed her. In those jeans, he'd have followed her anywhere. She wasn't built like the women he was used to seeing. He'd seen more than his share of hard bodies and they didn't do much for him. Not that she wasn't attractive; Allison had a body that could drive any man wild. Her full shapely legs went all the way up to heaven. She had arms that could squeeze the heart out of man. He especially liked the way her slender waist accentuated her more than ample breasts. He could just imagine how they would feel in his hands.

"Will? You all right?"

"Yeah, why?" Will cleared his throat and turned away from her. He set the bag of kibbles on the ground and untucked his T-shirt. If this morning held any indication, he'd be spending the entire week with his shirttails out. No point in advertising the effect she had on his manhood.

Allison bent down and opened the latch on a small cage under a table. A small gray ferret scurried out. She scooped it up and it wrapped itself around her neck. The animal returned her small kisses with soft chirping noises.

"How come he gets kisses while you're on the clock?" Will teased.

"I'm the boss. I decide who I want to kiss."

"Well, isn't that special?"

"Goodness, Will. You sound like you're jealous." Allison flashed him a smile that told him she saw too much.

"Me, jealous of a ferret with half a tail? Not a chance. I can hold my own. So, how'd he lose his tail anyway?" Will stepped a little closer to Allison. The ferret lifted his head and hissed.

"Stubby, you stop that. Will is our friend." She scratched the animal's little head and he nuzzled her neck.

"Stubby, how appropriate." Will took another step and again Stubby hissed. "I think it might take a little while for him to get used to me."

"Are you afraid of ferrets?"

"Of course not. I just don't have much experience with them."

"I guess." Allison eyed him warily and he smiled. He really wasn't afraid; he just didn't like little hairy things. He'd never even owned a hamster, or any rodent for that matter.

Allison led him around the rest of the shelter and introduced him to the other animals. He was okay with the dogs and he could tolerate the cats, but he still wasn't too sure about Stubby.

The ferret followed behind them at what Will hoped was a safe distance. They had two more animals to feed and then the real work would begin. Or so Allison had told him.

Will leaned down and peered into the doghouse. The sign over the door said Tippy. "So this is the infamous—"

"Let it go, Will." Allison smacked his arm playfully and the contact set his nerves on edge.

"Fine. You're the boss. So, why does Tippy have a real home and the other animals are caged?"

Allison sat on the ground and made clicking noises. After several minutes, her noises were met with a stream of chattering from inside the house.

"Come here, honey." The raccoon poked his nose

out of the small doorway. He spied Allison and scurried out into her lap.

Will watched. It amazed him how she connected with the animals. They all trusted her without hesitation. She had a special quality and he understood how easy it was to put trust in her. He'd done it.

"Sit down next to me, Will."

Will did as she instructed. Cautiously, the small raccoon sniffed in his direction. After Tippy circled him several times the creature crawled into his lap. "Tippy is much friendlier than Stubby. She's kinda cute, too."

Tippy stood up in Will's lap and inspected his face. Nervous didn't begin to describe how Will felt. All he could see were the sharp claws on Tippy's one front paw.

"Relax, Will. She's making sure you're okay. Tippy is very protective and I think her own injury makes her maternal."

Allison watched Tippy sniff curiously around Will's face, then move around to the side of his neck. Tippy reached up and gave Will's newly pierced earlobe a flick.

"Ouch. Okay little one, that ear's off limits."

Allison clicked her tongue. "Imagine a grown man getting an earring."

"Yeah, funny the things grown men do to please the women in their lives."

Allison stood up and stretched her hand out to Will. "Come on. We've got work to do." A bolt of something close to lightning shot through Allison when their hands made contact.

The roughness of his palm scratched against hers, but not undesirably so. She'd have to make a point to avoid physical contact with him if she intended to get any work done.

"We have an eight o'clock appointment. And I think I'll let you handle it."

Will looked at her, his eyebrow raised in question. "Do you really think it's a good idea to set me loose on the animal world so soon in my new career?"

"You'll be fine. Trust me." What a silly thing to say. Why should he trust her?

A car horn blasted outside and Allison went out to greet her customers. Will followed behind her. "Good morning, Katie. Hi, Lizzie."

"Hi, Allison. I'm so glad you suggested this. I hate giving Hoyden a bath. She's such a pest with the water."

"What's all this about?"

Everyone turned to face Will. He stood in what could only be described as a manly stance. A smile tugged at Allison's lips as she took in the brooding expression on his face. His long sturdy legs were spread slightly and he held his arms folded across his powerful looking chest.

"Hoyden is our first customer of the day. You're going to give her a bath and brush her out."

"I'm what? This wasn't part of the deal. I am here to get to know the animals that stay here."

"Will, you don't *have* to do this. You're here so I can show you how important this place is to the animals *and* the community."

"How does giving my own dog a bath qualify for that?"

"Truthfully, it doesn't, she just happens to be our first customer. A lot of Brasselton's residents are old and they need help with their animals. We do a lot of house calls and this is just good practice for later today."

Allison smiled and hoped he didn't ask her outright about their next job. No such luck.

"What would that be?" Will took a step toward her. She stood her ground.

"We have to go to the other side of town and give Mrs. Parker's Dalmatian a bath and flea dip." Allison tried not to smile, but the expression on Will's face was priceless. His mouth dropped open and his eyebrows shot up.

"A Dalmatian? That's as bad as Hoyden."

"Does this mean you're throwing in the towel?" Allison hoped not. No matter how silly her plan, she wanted to spend this time with him. Her reasons definitely qualified as more personal than business, but she refused to dwell on the wrong or right of that issue.

"I guess we'd better get started, Hoyden." Will took the leash from Lizzie, flashing all the women a weak grin before leading the dog toward the building.

"Will, the shampoo is on the shelf over the tub. Make sure you get all of the soap off her before you dry her or she'll get tangles in her fur."

Will didn't stop and his only sign of acknowledgment was a quick wave of his hand. Allison, Katie, and Lizzie lined up outside the window to watch Will.

"Al, are you gonna tell him he should do Hoyden outside?"

Allison smiled. "No."

"Allison, you are wicked." Lizzie giggled softly.

"Yep, I am."

Will spent ten minutes trying to coax the retriever into jumping up into the tub on her own. Hoyden wasn't the least bit cooperative. Finally, he attempted to scoop her up. Hoyden led him on a merry chase around the room. Will's saving grace came in the form of the leash dragging along behind the dog. He stomped on it and the animal stopped fast.

"All right, you beast, work with me here. This isn't about business anymore. It's about male pride."

Hoyden ran her tongue up the side of Will's face. "Good, if you love me you'll let me do this." Finally, Will lifted Hoyden up into the metal tub and turned on the faucet. He attached the short hose and began spraying the dog down.

Hoyden barked and yipped at the hose. She bit at the spray nozzle and successfully entangled herself in the length of the hose.

"No, Hoyden! Don't do it." Before Will could cover himself Hoyden shook with enough force to soak him from the waist up.

"Oh my. They're making a horrible mess, Al. I can't believe you are making him do this." Allison didn't say anything. She simply smiled her acknowledgment.

They turned their attention back to Will when they heard the string of obscenities fill the air. Hoyden stood in the tub covered with bubbles from tip to tail. Will looked hilarious with a stream of lather dripping down the center of his face.

"Look, pooch, if you don't want a bath just say so and we're out of here."

Hoyden must have taken that for her cue, because she leaped out of the tub and headed for the door.

"Oh no you don't you spoiled brat. You are gonna get back in that tub and finish what we started." He lunged for the dog only to slide short of grasping her collar. Hoyden darted under a table and slid across the room to end up sitting next to the tub. Will slowly crept toward her. "Come on, Sweetie. Let me get those bad bubbles off you." He reached for her, but she dashed away again.

Allison laughed and decided the time had come to step in before Hoyden did serious damage to Will and his ego.

Allison opened the door and moved to step in. "Okay, it looks like you could use a–"

Hoyden saw her chance and bolted out the opening.

"Oh my."

Will lie at her feet looking up at her. "Oh my, is

right."

Allison grinned. "Don't just lay there; we've got to catch her."

"You let her out. You catch her."

Hoyden ran around the yard. Every few steps she stopped to shake off a few more of the troublesome bubbles. Allison kept her eye on the escapee while she pulled Will up off the ground.

Hoyden dodged between the main building and the shed. Allison went one way and Will circled around to the back. When she reached the corner of the building she saw Hoyden sitting under a huge tree. She panted and stared in their direction. When Will advanced on her, Hoyden remained perfectly still.

"Go very slow, Will, or you'll spook her. A little bit further and you can grab her collar." Will lunged.

Hoyden's soft fur slipped through his fingers. She barked and ran for the front of the building. When Will looked up, he saw Allison, Katie, and Lizzie all standing over him.

"Don't any of you say a word."

"Are–" Allison started.

"Not one!" Will stood and stomped after the dog.

"I'm the owner here. I am the one in control. I have managed to design and build huge buildings all over America, I'm certain I can bathe a dog."

Hoyden eyed him as he approached. Will tried to predict which direction she would bolt. When she jumped, he moved the same direction. Confused, Hoyden turned and headed toward the truck. Allison ran forward and cut her off. Will smiled as Hoyden jumped into the bed of the truck. Her paws slid across the truck bed and she hit the cab with a thud.

"I've got you now. You overgrown pain in the–"

"She's gonna go over the side, Will."

"No she won't," Will said matter-of-factly. "She'll go up, but the big baby is afraid to jump back down."

Will sat on the open tailgate and stared at the matted mess of fur he called a pet.

Will caught a mouth full of freezing water when he opened it to yell. "Yeeow!"

Allison held the trigger on the hose and sprayed both dog and owner.

"Oh, Al, I can't believe you did that." Katie stood with her hand over her mouth. Lizzie stood next to her doubled over, tears of laughter rolling down her cheeks.

"I had to get the soap off. You know that concentrated stuff will give them both a rash if it stays on too long."

"Oh, but, girlfriend, you could have warned him."

"And miss all the fun?"

"You know Al, I'm gonna have to get you back for this." Will's first reaction had been anger, but when he looked up and saw her green eyes glowing with mischief, he let it go. He liked seeing her smile. Even at his expense.

Will spent the rest of the day following Allison around. At a few minutes before five o'clock, Allison handed him a pair of clippers. The day had been pretty quiet once Lizzie had taken Hoyden home. Allison had kept him busy moving supplies from the shed into the main building. Thank goodness for fitness centers or his muscles would be screaming in protest.

Several times he'd stopped to rest and found Allison staring at him. How did she expect him to concentrate on his work when she kept looking at him with those eyes? If the first day held any indication, it would be a long week.

"Well, I'd say it's time to finish up for the day." Allison picked up her keys and purse and headed for the door. "Let's go."

"Cool." Will set the clippers down on the counter and moved toward the door.

"You may want to pick those back up." She chuckled aloud at his confused expression. "What's wrong?"

"I thought we were finished."

"No, I said we needed to finish up. We have to stop and clip some toenails before we head home. I hope you weren't expecting banker's hours."

Will coughed and sputtered. "Of course not. I must not have been paying attention. My mistake."

It took less than ten minutes to reach their last client's house and another forty for Will to get the dog's nails clipped. Allison sat back and watched with total amazement at how wet one dog could get a man. Will would have to shower twice to get all the dog slobber off him. The thought of him in the shower set her hormones into action. The ride home dragged on for way too long, and Allison could only think of a cold shower. Anything to clear her mind of the images Will evoked.

◀ Six ▶

Once in her driveway, Will said his good-byes and hurried across the street. She reached down to pull her keys from her purse. A moment later, the phone began ringing. After fumbling with the lock and shoving the door open, Allison raced through her house trying to catch the telephone. As usual, it stopped ringing as she slipped to a halt next to the three-legged table in the hallway.

Katie's voice echoed through the house from the answering machine in the kitchen. "Just checking in, I wanted to see how the afternoon went."

Allison laughed and decided to shower before returning her calls.

The cool water rolled down her back, but did little to ease the tension. She leaned her head against the shower wall and closed her eyes. Every muscle in her body tensed when Will's image crowded in. She reached down and turned the hot water all the way off. At least this way she wouldn't know if the chills coursing through her were from the water, or her not so pure thoughts of her new neighbor.

Four day later, she found herself in the exact same

spot, trembling against the chilly water, wishing she could have him, and refusing to admit she wanted him. This time when the phone rang she got to it before it stopped. Dripping all over the plush carpet of her bedroom, she started at the sound of Will's voice. Five minutes later, she'd agreed to a shopping spree in the Fort Worth Stockyards the next day. She'd pick Lizzie and him up around eleven o'clock.

Lizzie was full of smiles and conversation the next day as they drove through Fort Worth. Allison found herself swept up in the youngsters retelling of a book she'd just read. Oh, what she'd give for even half the girl's enthusiasm and energy.

She and Will followed Lizzie across the parking lot and onto the brick streets of the Stockyards. They window-shopped for a bit before finding their way into a western-wear store.

Some time later, Will stepped out of the dressing room and frowned at his cohorts. Lizzie and Allison waited in the foyer; hands over their mouths trying to suppress their laughter. He turned and stared at his reflection in the three-way mirror. The skintight jeans clung to his legs like bark to a tree. The longest, leanest most excruciatingly sexy legs she'd ever seen. The red and black checked shirt clashed with his bright, exhilarating personality and from the expression on his face, the boots on his feet squeezed his toes to the point of agony.

Will took a few steps and scrunched up his face.

"Well, you definitely look like you belong in

Brasselton." Allison coughed into her hand and he suspected it covered a laugh. "But you look good."

"Uncle Will, you look like–well, you look like– who's that old man in all the cowboy movies?"

Soft air hissed out of Will's ego at the reference to age.

"Oh, you mean Will Rogers?" Allison choked out the words as she watched Will's face turn a wild array of colors.

"He has a museum or something named after him. I saw it on the news. It's here in Fort Worth and they do all the big animal shows there." Lizzie waved her arms around in front of her. "Oh, oh, his horse's name is Bullet."

"Trigger."

"What?" Allison and Lizzie asked in unison.

"Trigger." Will snapped at them. "Will Roger's horse's name was Trigger." Will, nearing the end of his patience, turned to go back into the dressing room. "I've had enough." He'd almost made it into the cubicle before Allison stopped him. Her hand rested lightly on his sleeve and he looked down at her. The shock of electricity her every touch caused still jarred him senseless.

"Trigger was the name of Roy Roger's horse. Not Will. I'm not sure what Will's horse's name was."

"Is there a point to all this?" Will sighed, his shoulders sagging.

"Roy's dog's name was Bullitt."

Will glared down at her.

"I'm sorry we picked on you." She moved her hand up to rest against his cheek and she smiled at him. "You do look pretty damn sexy in the outfit. I'd be proud to boot scoot with you any day."

Will covered her hand with his and then turned her palm against his lips. "You're only saying that because I'm your ride home."

"I don't think so. I drove." Al grinned up at him, her eyes sparkling under the track lighting. "And your arrogance will cost you."

"Oh?"

"You're buying lunch." Allison pinched his cheek and stepped out of the dressing room area. His grumbling voice followed her out into the store.

"Is Uncle Will mad at me?" Not so much of an ounce of true concern showed anywhere in Lizzie's face. In fact, Allison thought, the teenager looked a little too amused for her own good. Her pale blue eyes sparkled with mischief.

Finally, Will stepped out of the dressing room wearing his own clothes and looking quite content. "You two are going to have to find some other helpless Podunk boy to make over. The yuppie look works for me and I plan on sticking with it." He rubbed his hands down the front of his shirt, smoothing out imaginary wrinkles.

Allison watched him intently. Solid muscles flexed and rippled along the length of his arms, the curves along his washboard stomach nestled against the inside of his cotton shirt. Allison sighed. The good

Lord had really outdone himself when he created this man. A near perfect body, a sparkling personality, and lips to die for. Experience had given her that bit of information. Their first encounter in his back yard had left her unable to resist him. No matter how hard she tried, she couldn't seem to keep her mind–or her hands–off him.

"Are you two shopaholics ready to hit the streets?" He walked behind them, but stepped ahead to open the door leading out onto the Stockyard's sidewalk. People milled around, tourists snapped pictures, and cars crawled past. Allison loved the old historic area, and yet never found time to enjoy the surroundings.

"I think we should hit the craft shops and see what we can find. I have a brand new shelf to fill up." Lizzie smiled and strolled ahead. Her head turned from side to side, taking in all the sights. Each time she spotted a young man who looked close to her age, her shoulders rolled back and her chin went up.

Allison leaned over and whispered in Will's ear. "I think she's checking out the future cowboys."

"Well, she can just cut it out. It will be at least ten years before she has to worry about it." Will's brows slid together and a crease formed across his forehead. "I don't have any intention of letting some young stud get his hands on Lizzie."

"Oh, simmer down. She's a good girl and most of the boys in Brasselton are well-raised."

A crowd of teenagers brushed between them and Will reached out and took Allison's hand. A shiver shook her hard enough to draw Will's attention. "You okay, Al?" He tightened his grip on her hand and slowed his pace.

Allison's cheeks flushed and she lowered her head. "I'm fine, just a chill."

Lizzie stopped in front of a T-shirt shop and read some of the phrases aloud. *'They've fallen and they can't get up',* graced the top of a white shirt. Allison and Lizzie laughed when Will questioned the little old lady under the caption.

"I just don't get it."

Allison and Lizzie both poked out their chests and laughed.

"Gravity isn't always our friend," Allison chimed.

Will's brows shot up and his cheeked heated. "Oh."

The trio laughed until tears rolled down all their faces.

Several doors down, Lizzie pushed her way into another western apparel store. Reluctantly, Will followed. When the two women filled their arms with enough merchandise to clothe a small country, he found a chair and plopped down into it. He whistled and nodded accordingly as the two women paraded past him in a variety of outfits. Once they'd paid for everything and loaded his arms, they headed back out into the crowd.

"Well, if you two don't have anything else to do, I think we should eat."

Allison opened her mouth to agree, but never got

the words out. Lizzie stood in the middle of a closed off street waving her arms and pointing at something. Allison looked around a tall man and saw what drew the crowd's attention. An old authentic looking cowboy stood next to a huge sleepy looking longhorn. The animal's head hung low and he stood motionless as child after child crawled on and off his back. Will snickered as a grown man in plaid shorts crawled up and perched himself on the animal's back.

"I can't believe they let people get on that thing."

Lizzie pulled her camera out of her bag and pushed Will toward the beast.

"Oh no you don't. I'm not going near that thing."

"Oh, don't be a baby. Look at it, he hasn't moved in ten minutes." As if to reinforce her encouraging theory, the longhorn opened its mouth and yawned.

"Uncle Will, please. I want a picture of you on its back for my scrap book." Lizzie looped her arm through his and fluttered her eyelashes. "Pretty please."

Allison took his other arm and joined Lizzie's urging. "I would love a copy of it for my own personal use."

"Oh, and what the–heck does that mean?" Will stepped away from his companions and considered dashing across the street and away from the crazy women obviously determined to make his life a nightmare, Lizzie by being a teenager and Allison by being a woman. He didn't stand a chance. He looked over to see them both staring at him with faces too beautiful to resist. Lizzie had already managed to perfect her mother's *give me what I want* look and Allison had eyes warm enough to melt the arctic zone. "But it's a big bull."

"No, Uncle Will, it's a longhorn." She sighed her frustration at his apparent ignorance. "Besides, look at it. The thing hasn't so much as moved."

"Yeah, Uncle Will, what are you afraid of?"

"I'm a man damn it. I'm not afraid of anything, much less a stupid cow." The grunting response he was only considering shot out of his mouth before he could finish thinking it. At least that's why he figured the crowd stopped and stared at him. What little self-respect he'd managed to hold onto slipped out of his grasp and disappeared into a deep abyss of nothingness somewhere out of his reach.

He took a hesitant step toward the docile creature then paused. He waited for the longhorn to sense his fear and charge him, but it didn't. It did however raise its head and stare directly at him. Will, determined not to let a challenge go unheeded, took several more steps. The crowd around him hushed and waited for something to happen. When he finally made it to the animal, the crowd had closed in around him. Small children teased and taunted him, calling him a sissy and laughing.

"Look, Mommy, that man is 'fraid of the moo cow."

Will looked at the blond-haired blue-eyed child and thanked God he wasn't his. "I am not afraid of him."

"Are too."

"Am not."

"Too."

"Not."

Allison stepped between them and gave Will a playful shove. "Don't make me separate you two."

"He started it," Will whined. He leaned down and whispered in Al's ear. "Are you really going to let me do this?"

She responded by kissing his cheek. "I wouldn't have it any other way." She swatted him on the bottom, chuckled, and stepped back. "Now ride 'em cowboy."

After setting his packages on the ground by Al, Will shot her a glare.

The crowd whispered and he knew how it felt to be a condemned man. The animal's keeper stepped up and mumbled a few quick instructions to him. Knowing the full impact of defeat, Will stepped up onto the podium beside the longhorn. He grabbed the horn and hoisted himself into the saddle. The animal shifted its weight and Will's stomach lurched.

"Easy, boy. Give him a minute to get used to your weight."

Will took a deep breath and held it. The beast shifted again and Will let the breath out–a little too quickly. He closed his eyes and waited for his balance to settle. "My weight? He weighs ten times what I do, and I need to worry about him."

Without warning, electronic flashes blinked around him. The blinding lights left spots for him to sort out. Then it hit him, like a ton of bricks, if they were upsetting him, imagine how the moo-cow felt. A split second later, he found out. The usually docile and lazy longhorn took a step, then another. Children laughed and tried to move toward the animal as their parents pulled them away, scurrying out of potential harm's way. The keeper shouted commands, all of which went unheeded. Mr. Moo Cow was stampeding. Okay, he wasn't moving fast enough to do any real damage, but the big ol' hunk of beef was tooling along through the Stockyards.

"Will, jump off." Allison rushed toward him, her expression switching between amusement and concern.

"No, don't jump. Just hang on, I'll git him to stop."

Will held on, the longhorn walked, and the crowd cheered. The louder they cheered, the faster they moved. Fortunate for him, he thought, the animal wasn't inclined to go too far too fast.

Crowds along the sidewalks stopped to stare at him. They'd made it almost to the train tracks when the beast finally decided to take a rest. His owner rushed up and tossed a rope around its neck. He nuzzled the animal and whispered softly to it.

Will waited almost a half a second before he swung his khaki clad leg over and jumped off the beast. Allison stood off in the center of a crowd staring in his direction. He couldn't decide if he wanted to run over and hug her, or smack the amused look off her face. He chose to keep his distance. Not that he had any choice in the matter. A Fort Worth mounted police officer approached him and asked for a report. Will told him what happened as quickly as he could. All he wanted was to get home, out of the public eye.

"Uncle Will, I think you've earned a reprieve." Lizzie took his hand in hers and tugged him toward a restaurant across the street. "Al and I are going to buy you lunch."

They stopped at the truck and dropped off all their purchases before heading toward the restaurants.

"You deserve a break today." Al took his other hand and the trio crossed the street. She turned her face away when the crowd in the eatery applauded when they walked in the door. If it wasn't all so funny, she might feel guilty for goading him into the ride in the first place.

A tall man in jeans and a cowboy hat approached them. "That was quite ride you had there. The customers all agreed we oughta give you lunch free, in exchange for the show." He extended his hand and Will shook it.

"Thanks, some folks will do anything for a free meal."

The crowd laughed and applauded again. Five minutes later, they were seated at a table being served heaping barbecue sandwiches.

All through the meal children pointed and parents chuckled. Would this day never end?

Will managed to get through the rest of their outing without getting into any more trouble. They headed back to Allison's truck a little before dusk.

After shifting their packages into the truck bed and getting Lizzie situated, they headed home. Will spent most of the trip home staring out the tinted window. It wasn't until they reached the Brasselton city limits he spoke.

"Al, I want to thank you."

She looked over at him. His expression looked serious and it made her a little nervous. "For what?" Her grip on the steering wheel tightened. *Settle down, girl, what could be wrong?*

"Today was the first time I've seen Lizzie really enjoy herself. It means a lot to her that you two have become friends." He turned and looked at Lizzie who was snuggled in a corner of the truck bed.

The air whizzed out of her and Allison stared straight ahead. So, that was the way of it. This was all for Lizzie. "No problem, I like Lizzie a lot. She's a great kid." She turned to find Will staring at her.

"I don't know how I'm going to handle her on my own. I don't know anything about kids, especially girl kids."

Al forced a smile. "Well, if you need advice, you know where to find me. I'll help Lizzie any way I can."

"Al, are you okay? You suddenly seem a little distracted."

"You don't have to thank me for doing something I enjoy. It's not like it's a duty to be with–Lizzie."

Will sighed. "I know, but I didn't want you to think I–oh, never mind."

They rode the rest of the way through town in

silence. Al pulled into her driveway and stepped out of the truck. When Will moved to carry her packages, she grabbed them away from him. "I can manage; thanks."

Will stuffed his hands into his pockets and didn't say anything.

"Lizzie, I'll see you in the morning. We'll walk into town and see what kind of trouble we can get into." After a quick hug Al headed toward her front door, leaving a very dazed and confused Will standing by the road.

"Uncle Will, what did you say to her?" Lizzie challenged.

His eyes grew wide. "What did I say?" He jerked his hands out of his pockets and unlocked the door. "I thanked her for spending the day with you and then she just clammed up."

"With me?" Lizzie's hands waved in the air and she sputtered and mumbled under her breath. "Men!"

"What?" He turned and looked at his niece who was having what could only be described as a hissy fit.

She stood with her arms folded across her chest, then unfolded them and waved them in the air as her mouth opened and closed without making a sound. She spun to walk away, then turned back.

"Did you tell her how much *you* enjoyed the day?" With hands on her hips, Lizzie waited for his reply. "Well?"

"I always have a good time with her."

"So, you tell her that every time you see her?"

Lizzie pushed past him into the house. "How will she know if you don't tell her?"

"Are you telling me she's mad because I didn't tell her I had a good time?" He closed the front door behind him and stepped into the front room.

"Well–"

He plopped down on the couch and thought about it. Wasn't that one of the things Marty always complained about? Coop always assumed she knew. *Oh boy.* He rested his head back on the sofa and sighed, again. I guess I have some 'splaining to do. "Hey, Lizzie, I'll be back in a while. If you need anything I'll be across the street trying to get my foot out of my mouth."

"Uncle Will?" Lizzie took his hands in hers and looked up at him. "Don't mess this up, you and Al are too perfect together."

"Lizzie, we're just friends."

"I know, but if you play your cards right, you might let her figure out ya'll belong together."

Will stared down into Lizzie's eyes. She was everything her mother had been, beautiful, intelligent, loving, and too nosey and outspoken for her own good. "It's a good thing I love you as much as I do."

"Yeah, a good thing for both of us." She kissed him on his cheek and scurried upstairs. Head hanging and lip poking out, Will walked across the street. How could he admit to Al that he had assumed she knew he wanted to be with her?

Allison took her time getting to the door. She

didn't know why Katie didn't let herself in; that was the point of her having a key. The sheer red robe flapped behind her as she walked. She tugged at the hem of her long white tank top as she flung the door open. "Good heavens, why didn't you just come in already?" Her eyes lingered on the sight before her and she waited for the herd of rhinos to waltz into her gaping mouth.

"Well, to be honest, I wasn't invited."

"Then why are you here?" *Now is that any way to talk to a man who does the things to your body he does?* Allison waited for lightning to strike her, but her luck held and the good Lord left her to get out of her own mess.

"Maybe I shouldn't be. I won't bother you."

"You already have." *Boy have you.* "I mean, you're already here, so what do you want?" Blast, why couldn't she say what she meant?

"Allison, are you okay?" He took a step toward her and the heat of his body scorched her. "I mean, I know you are mad at me, but–"

"What on earth makes you think I am mad at anyone?" She clutched the doorknob a little tighter.

"Maybe it's the cool goodbye I got earlier, or the hostile greeting I just got." His sad expression distracted her for a brief moment.

"It's not that. You just caught me in my–" She looked down to find her bare legs poking from beneath a decidedly too short shirt. Her robe was tucked under her arms, leaving her darn near totally exposed.

"Glory," he said.

"Glory, what?

"Standing there in all your glory." His eyes scanned the length of her body, lingering a moment longer at her chest before moving up to her face. "That's quite an outfit you've put together."

"Oh my." She grabbed for the opening of her robe and struggled to pull it together in the front. Will took her hand and kept her from doing it.

"I wanted to tell you what a wonderful time I had today."

"Yes, I think Lizzie enjoyed it."

Will shook his head. "She did, but I wanted you to know, I did too." Will looked straight into her eyes and their gazes held. His hand slipped from hers and traveled up her arm, coming to rest on her shoulder. "I can't remember the last time I enjoyed shopping."

Allison held her ground, but her knees threatened to give out. His thumb rubbed along her jaw line, causing irreparable damage to her senses.

"I can't remember the last time I enjoyed anything."

His breath traveled across her cheek and down into her soul. Everything in her mind told her to close the door and head back to the shower, but his touch, the whisper of his breath, and her pure and simple desire for him held her in place. She closed her eyes and lifted her head toward him. His lips touched hers at the same moment she opened her eyes. His mouth barely brushed hers, but her reaction multiplied the intensity. She grabbed the collar of his shirt and tugged him closer. Pressing his chest against hers, they melted into one.

His hand moved from her shoulder to caress her neck. The gentle tug on her hair released something primal and animalistic in her. Clawing at his arms and shoulders, she dragged him into the house and kicked the door closed.

They both gasped for air as their lips pressed together, only coming apart long enough to nibble or bite at the other's. His hands burned a trail along her back and down to her waist, kneading and tormenting her. Her hands took on their own direction as she pulled and tugged at his shirt.

Finally, the hem of his shirt came loose from his pants and she jerked it over his head. She looked up to find him staring down at her, his eyes glazed over and bright with anticipation.

"Am I going too slow for you?" His tone held a note of teasing, but at the same time his hands fumbled with his belt.

"Not at all." She pushed his hands away and undid the metal buckle herself. She pulled him by the waistband into the living room and shoved him into a chair. She stood above him, still wearing her shirt and robe. She pulled the silk back off her shoulders as provocatively as she could, and let it fall to the floor.

She ran her tongue across her lips and prayed for control, while Will sat in the chair, his hands clenched on the arms, every visible muscle in his body taught and ready to snap. How could any man look so handsome? The dark hair covering his chest glistened with perspiration. The scent of him drifted up around her and muddled her thoughts. He never took his eyes off her.

"Allison–"

Before he could say anything else, she knelt down in front of him. She pushed him back, tugged at his open waistband, and carefully pulled his pants down. When he lifted himself so she could take them off, she pressed her lips to his stomach.

"Al, don't–" His words cut off as she dragged her tongue down to just above the top of his boxers. She looked up to find his head thrown back against the chair and his eyes closed.

Without hesitation, she slipped his shorts down his legs and tossed them across the room. She leaned back and openly admired him. Fine dark hair covered most of his body, sensuously enhancing his perfect physique. She moved forward and flicked her tongue across his hardened nipple. Slowly, she drew a wet circle and exhaled. His entire body shook. He lifted a shaky hand and thrust his fingers into her damp hair. Pulling her closer, he arched against her.

Allison took his nipple between her teeth and gently plucked at the tender flesh.

"That's not fair," he rasped.

"What's fair?" She dropped her hands down to his ankles and slowly trailed them up the outside of his legs. When she reached his thighs she hesitated, but only long enough for him to take a deep breath. "If I

Karen L. Syed

didn't know any better, I'd say you're glad to be here."
She took one hand and moved it over to cover him.

When all he did was mumble something she didn't
understand, she grew bolder.

She lowered her head and let her tongue dance
across the supple skin of his erection.

Will held himself completely still. Her mouth on
him made him feel things he'd never imagined. He
prayed for self-control and release, not quite yet
though. He didn't want her to stop.

It took only minutes for him to realize he had to
stop her. He refused to let her end this before he'd had
his turn on her. "Al, stop."

She rolled her eyes up to look at him. "Hmm?"

"Not like this, Al." He took her by the arms and
pulled her up into his lap. She put a leg on either side
of him and leaned against his chest. Again, their lips
met. Nothing could have stopped him from taking her
at this point, but he wanted to make sure she got as
much pleasure as she gave.

While their lips fused with a desperate sense of
urgency, he lifted against her. A soft sigh escaped
between them as he pressed his arousal against her.
Her nails dug into his shoulders before moving up into
his hair.

Her body tensed as he slipped his hand between
her legs. Moving aside the thin fabric, he met the proof
of her feelings. A soft "Oh," slipped out of her mouth
as his finger slipped inside her. Within seconds he had
her rocking back and forth against him. With each

movement he felt her growing closer to release, but not yet. He pulled his hand free and wrapped his arms around her.

She fell against him, clinging. After several minutes, they reluctantly parted, but only far enough to look at one another. He touched her cheek with his fingertip. "I don't want to make love to you in this chair."

"I don't care where; I just want you to make love to me."

Will scooted forward in his chair, but held her when she started to get up.

He wrapped her legs around his waist and stood up. Slowly, Will walked toward the staircase.

They made it as far as the bottom step before they lost control.

Allison held onto him with one hand and struggled to remove her shirt with the other. Turning around, Will pressed her back against the wall and helped her pull the shirt over her head.

Frantic to touch and taste every inch of her, Will pressed his hands to her bottom and lifted her so he could get his mouth on her nipple. He struggled for breath as the peak grew against his tongue, driving away all rational thought.

What was happening? He wondered at the intensity of his feelings at this woman he couldn't get enough of, as she writhed against him, pushing and moaning into his ear.

Soft skin warmed the palms of his hands as she

squirmed. When her tongue slipped into his ear, he grabbed the flimsy fabric of her lacy underwear and yanked until the seam gave. He pulled on them until he was able to slip them off one leg. When the warmth of their separate bodies met–flesh against flesh–the fight ended.

With one swift motion, he slipped inside her.

The ecstasy of the moment catapulted him into another dimension. With one hand on her back and the other on the wall behind her, Will pushed into her, again and again. Driving all of the things he felt for her as deeply as he could. Each stroke exploded into another erotic declaration of something unspoken.

"Will, I'm–"

Their mouths joined again as their bodies touch off a wave of pure and untainted rapture. Her heart beat against his and their breath mingled in the first seconds of relief.

Allison clung to him, possessively. He pulled her as tight against him as the position would allow. When the quivers of release began to subside, his knees grew weak. Fearing he'd drop her and fall himself, he lowered them both down onto the step and leaned back. The scratchy carpet tickled the back of his neck as he let his head rest.

"I'm glad we didn't make love in the chair."

Will opened his eyes to find Allison smiling down at him. When he opened his mouth to speak, she quieted him with a kiss. A kiss that set everything in motion again. Fire raced through his body and sparked another round of tormenting desire. This time, he'd do it right. He'd get up off the floor and carry her to the bed, if it took him all night. He'd almost gathered the strength when the front door opened.

"Oh my." Katie and Allison mumbled the words at the same moment.

Katie stepped back out and slammed the door.

Will's head dropped back onto the step with a painful thud.

"Good lord, Will get dressed. I have to stop her." Allison tried to stand up, but Will stopped her.

"This isn't finished." He kissed her soundly on the mouth and pushed her up. "Now get off me before someone thinks I've been less than a gentleman."

Allison's mouth dropped open, but nothing came out. She looked at him. That was all, just looked.

Allison tugged her robe around her and jerked open the front door. She stared out toward the road, looking for Katie's car. A cough beside her made her jump. Katie stood beside the door, her passkey held out in front of her. "I think I ought to give this back."

Allison laughed. At first, it was a nervous laugh then it turned into a full-blown giggle fest. "No, keep it; I'll hang a bra on the door next time."

They were still giggling when Will stepped out the front door. He took one look at Allison's short robe and frowned. She looked down and realized his thoughts. What would the neighbors think? Not that she cared, or that they could see. The hedges around the house and the fact that it was dark out made it next to impossible to see onto her front porch.

"Don't you think you should go inside, before someone sees you?" The possessive tone in his voice flattered, and at the same time annoyed her.

"As a matter of fact, I guess I should go inside." She stepped toward the door, but stopped. Katie pushed past her and went in.

"Remember what I said, Al." He pulled her into his arms and kissed her soundly. A little too soundly.

"Hmm?"

"This is not over." He let her go and she stumbled back a step.

Regaining her composure, she straightened her back, took a deep breath, and smiled. "Count on it, stud." Then she left him standing on the front porch, this time it was his mouth hanging open. She laughed when she heard his parting comment.

"Yowsa, what a woman."

She watched him walk across the yard, whistling. When she turned around, Katie stood with her arms folded across her chest and her foot tapping on the carpet.

"What?"

"Don't you what me. He's been gone almost two minutes and you have not even made any effort to tell me every single detail, and don't you dare leave anything out."

Allison smiled and led her best friend into the kitchen by the hand, chattering a hundred miles an hour. Forty-five minutes later, and out of breath, Al leaned back in her chair.

"So, what you're telling me is you ravished your neighbor."

"Yeah, I guess I did. Who would have thunk it?"

"There may be hope for you yet."

Will dropped onto the bed and closed his eyes. He draped his hand over his eyes and knew it immediately to be a mistake. Her scent lingered on every part of his body. He felt like a sixteen-year-old boy.

"Uncle Will, did you get it all straightened out?"

Will shot upright so fast his head spun. He focused on Lizzie, his pure, sweet, and remarkably innocent niece standing in his bedroom doorway. Her face, beautiful and soft, held a breathtaking smile. "Yeah, we talked."

"I'll say." Lizzie covered her mouth and muffled her laugh with a forced cough.

"What's so funny?"

Lizzie walked into the room and touched the collar of his shirt. "That must have been some talk you two had. Al talked your shirt wrong side out." Lizzie leaned down and kissed him on the cheek. She lingered for a moment and then giggled again. "Is that Longing you're wearing?"

Will inhaled deep as Lizzie walked out of the room. Al's perfume wafted around him. Lizzie looked back once before closing his door. Okay, maybe not so innocent. He fell back on the bed and let his mind slip back to the events of the day. What a day. What a week. Will forced himself up off the bed and went to the window.

He had a great view of the front and side of Allison's house. He watched as Al hugged Katie goodbye. He considered going back over, but decided against it. The mere thought of being near her left him breathless and quaking. His cheeks warmed when she turned toward his house and waved. He waved back and headed straight for the shower. If he didn't cool off soon he'd be the first man to explode from desire. Ah, but what a way to go.

Saturday morning rolled around about six hours sooner than Al would have liked. Who the heck had the nerve to bang on her doorbell in the middle of the night? She opened her eyes and saw the sun streaming across her bed.

Sunlight meant morning, which also meant the culprit had to be Lizzie picking her up for their walk. She stumbled out of bed and grumbled her way to the door. Lizzie greeted her with a bear hug and a pastry.

"Good girl. Always come bearing gifts when waking the dead." Al took the fluffy glob of glaze and buried her mouth into it. "Pure heaven."

"Funny, that's exactly what Uncle Will said." Lizzie waggled her eyebrow and smiled.

"Is he going with us?" Part of her wanted him to; the other didn't think she could handle being within eyesight of him and not being able to touch him.

"Nope, he wolfed down the pastry, mumbled something about sore muscles, and crawled back under the covers."

Al understood. Every muscle in her body screamed when she'd stumbled out of bed. The thought of her legs wrapped around him brought more than a heated blush to her cheeks at the image she recalled. The thought of him in bed sent chills shooting through her body.

"You okay, Al? You don't look so good."

This kid is way too perceptive for her own good. "Yeah, I'm fine, hon." Al stepped back and ushered Lizzie into the living room. She choked when Lizzie picked up Will's boxer shorts off the floor. "Oh my."

"I guess I'll let you return these." She tossed them across the room and giggled.

"Those are–"

"Uncle Will's favorites." Lizzie gave Al a quick hug. "Don't worry, I won't tell anyone I know what happened."

"Whatever do you mean?" Allison asked innocently, then smiled. "You're way too young to be this smart."

"Mom and dad couldn't keep their hands off each other and they made sure I knew what was right and wrong at a very young age." Lizzie's expression grew sad and Al knew she was thinking about her parents.

"If you give me a minute, we can talk while we walk."

"I'd like that."

Allison ran up the stairs, stopping for a split second on the bottom step when she remembered Will sitting on it naked. She took a two-minute shower and was dressed and back downstairs in ten minutes. She filled a water bottle for each of them and added ice. When they stepped out onto the sidewalk her gaze went automatically to Will's bedroom window.

He raised his cup of coffee and smiled down at her.

Allison tried to concentrate on the soft breeze blowing the leaves around. For a change the sky offered no threat of rain. Of course in Texas that could change at a moment's notice.

She had considered driving into town, but they needed the exercise and she didn't want to deal with pulling the protective cover off the Mustang. She'd had her drive for the week.

The companionable silence suited her just fine. It gave her time to consider the relationship between her and Will.

Things had definitely taken an interesting turn.

A few blocks down the road Lizzie finally spoke. "Uncle Will thinks I'm still a kid. He got mad the other day because I said I wanted to go to the movies with a boy from town."

"Oh Lizzie, he doesn't think you're a kid. That's the whole problem. He knows you're not and he's afraid of losing you."

Lizzie thought about this for a minute. "Why

would he lose me? I like living with him. He's the greatest."

Al took her hand. "Yeah, he is, but he's still scared."

"Of what?" she asked. Then she understood. "He thinks I'm going to die, too."

Allison feared the direction their conversation had turned. She didn't have any idea how to comfort Lizzie, or Will. She could barely deal with her own grief. Eight years had passed since her mother's death and she still couldn't get past it. "I wish I could tell you this will all work out, but I don't know."

"I know he misses mom and so do I, but he can't live life being afraid every time I'm not with him."

"How'd you get to be so smart?" Al stroked the hair hanging down in Lizzie's eyes and wished she could help more. "Your uncle will come around, but this is all too new to him to let go."

Lizzie stared up at the sky as they walked. Her brows drawn together as she contemplated things. Al tried to make sense of the fluffy white clouds. Feeling silly, she decided to spend more time figuring out things that mattered. Like her feelings for Will Hoyt.

"Al, do you love my uncle?"

Al tripped over a pebble on the sidewalk and nearly landed on her face. She stopped and faced Lizzie. "What?"

"Well, I figure, if Uncle Will is busy being in love with you, he won't have time to be a pain in my neck."

"Lizzie, honey, that is a dreadful thing to say."

"No, it's not. I love him and I think you do too. Shouldn't you be happy? Shouldn't we all be happy?"

Al laughed and started walking again. "I wish I could believe you have my best interest at heart here."

"I do, I swear." Lizzie crossed her heart and held up three fingers in a Girl Scout salute.

"So, tell me about the boy. Is he cute? He doesn't drive does he?"

Lizzie rolled her eyes and Al laughed.

"Geez, now you sound like Uncle Will. Don't make me want both of you gone."

"I'm not that easy to get rid of. Besides, you need me."

Al and Lizzie spent most of the morning window-shopping. Al introduced Lizzie to the town's people and several of their children. When they got to the Pickett's gas station on the corner of Howard Road, Al suspected Lizzie already knew Jamie Pickett. Their eyes met across the small room and the temperature went up at least ten degrees. She waited outside while the two teenagers talked in hushed voices in the corner of the store.

"Lizzie, I think we should be getting back." She watched the small squeeze of Jamie's hand on Lizzie's, painting a soft rosy blush her cheeks.

They walked home in silence, both enjoying the quiet afternoon as they waved at the passing cars. Al loved the quiet closeness of Brasselton; it kept her from falling apart. So many things had gone wrong over the last ten years.

"Why do you live here, Al?" Lizzie stopped at the end of the sidewalk in front of her house.

"This is my home. I lived here as a child and came back–before my mother died." A twinge of pain pulled at her heart. "I came back to take care of her."

Lizzie's eyes filled with tears. Al took her hand and squeezed gently.

"I'm sorry."

"Hey, are you two gonna stand out here all day? I was starting to feel abandoned."

◀ Seven ▶

Al's heart lurched up into her throat at the sound of his raspy voice. Every inch of her body came alive with the memory of his touch. The recollection of his kiss on her lips sent her senses swirling.

Lizzie pecked him on the cheek and ran up the sidewalk and into the house, leaving Al and Will alone on the street. Thunder boomed in the afternoon sky as they stared into each other's eyes. "Are you busy for dinner tonight?" Will leaned toward her.

A few stray drops of rain fell, landing on the back of her exposed neck. "It's going to let loose soon. I should get home."

"You didn't answer me." He took her hand in his and stroked the top with his thumb. Her fingers tingled against his and she tried to think of a good excuse to refuse. Too much had happened over the last twenty-four hours and she needed time to think.

"I really don't think it would be a good idea."

"I'm sorry to hear that. I already started Lizzie's favorite meal and I know she'd like it if you'd join us." He brushed his lips across hers.

"So, this is all for her benefit?" Al asked nervously. His thumb brushed across the lips he'd just kissed. The rain fell harder, but neither moved. A flash of lightning streaked across' the dark and swiftly moving clouds, Al jumped. Will pulled her against him and wrapped his arms around her.

"You should get inside." He lowered his arms from around her and turned her toward her own house.

Al refused to be put off. "Answer my question." A longing stirred deep inside her. She wanted to be with Will, but not just because of Lizzie. For the first time in so very long, she wanted something more. She wanted him to desire her.

The feelings intensified as he stared down at her.

"No, Allison, it's not for Lizzie. I want you to come for dinner. I barely slept at all last night. I couldn't stop thinking about you and what happened. Since the moment I met you I've not stopped thinking about you." He lowered his head and kissed her. The rain fell and soaked them both, but did little to relieve the heat between them.

"What time do we eat?" Her words came out as more of a sigh than anything.

His lips barely allowed her to speak before kissing her again. For several long moments, they stood on the sidewalk in the rain, clinging to each other.

"I'll see you around six." He kissed her again then pushed her toward the street.

Allison ran across the street and fumbled with shaking fingers to open her front door. Once inside the house, she hit the button on her answering machine to listen to her messages. Will's voice filled the room.

"Hi, Al. I thought I would take a minute to tell you I was thinking about you. I'm sorry we got interrupted last night, but maybe it was for the best."

Al's heart dropped when he paused, but perked up again after his next words.

"I think maybe we should try a more conventional and less vigorous way to get to know each other. I have a plan. Talk to you later. Dinner is at six."

Arrogant beast. He'd assumed she'd say yes before he ever asked her. For a brief moment, she considered not going, but hey, she liked her nose, no sense in cutting it off to spite her face.

By the time four o'clock rolled around, she couldn't wait to leave. She cleaned out her refrigerator, rearranged her sock drawer, reapplied her lipstick–three times–and managed to kill thirty minutes. She sat in her kitchen debating whether or not to go over early. She decided she would wait until the final second, refusing to show her desperation to Will. Al leaned back in the chair and closed her eyes.

Will had made a few more trips out to the shelter since his first week. He claimed they were social calls, but each time he found something to do.

He and Tippy had become fast friends and Al couldn't help but wonder what he would do about the land. With their relationship growing in a different direction, she never found the right time to bring it up and he hadn't mentioned it either.

She pushed business out of her mind and let it dwell on other, more tantalizing ideas.

The feel of Will's hands caressing her neck sent chills along her spine. His hands slipped down her shoulders and moved around to her stomach. Every nerve in her body sparked to life and sent flickers of passion shooting out into the air. In a flash, he spun her around to face her, their lips coming together in a kiss of familiarity. Her hands slipped up and her fingers buried themselves deep into his hair. When they finally separated, Al struggled for air. "Oh my."

"Al, are you all right?"

Lizzie's voice filtered into range and Al opened her eyes. Lizzie stood over her, concern etched in her features. "I'm fine, sweetie." Al blushed.

"When I knocked on the screen door you didn't answer, then you started mumbling, oh my. I thought maybe you were sick."

The heat in her face increased. Now she was mumbling aloud while she daydreamed. What next? "I was just mumbling to myself." Suddenly, Al sat up straight and glanced at her watch.

Had she fallen asleep? Was she late? Oh Lord. Relief flooded through her when she saw she'd only been in la-la land for ten minutes or so. "What are you doing over here, Lizzie? Is everything okay?"

Lizzie sat down in one of the vacant chairs and sighed–a deep and exaggerated sigh of frustration. "Well, between me and you, no."

"No, what?"

Lizzie grumbled. "No, everything is not okay. I mean it is, but it isn't."

Al's experience with teenagers being as limited as it was, led her to grumble herself. "I don't understand."

"Me either."

"Lizzie, are you going to tell me what the problem is, or am I going to have to beat it out of you?"

Lizzie held up her hands and giggled. "It's Uncle Will."

Al bounced out of the chair and headed for the door. "Well, why didn't you tell me? What happened?" Al stopped when she heard Lizzie giggle behind her. "What–Lizzie?"

"That's exactly what I mean. Look at you. I mention his name and you go into a tizzy."

"Lizzie–"

"He's even worse. Do you know what he's doing right now?"

Probably wishing he hadn't become a single father to a teenage girl, if I had to guess. "I have no idea."

"He's trying to decide which shirt to wear so he doesn't look like a geek. He says he can't wear anything you've already seen him in."

Al experienced a momentary rush of panic. Had she already worn this outfit? Dang, she couldn't remember.

"Not you too." Lizzie stood up and began pacing the room. "I don't understand why this is such a big deal. We all know you like each other, but you haven't spent any time alone in a week."

"Will is trying to make sure you're okay. He doesn't want you to feel left out, or alone." *And we don't want to have any more opportunities to fall into bed until after we get to know each other better.*

"Sheesh, I'm not a kid, you know. I have stuff I wanna do and I can't because you two keep making me baby-sit."

Al wondered if all teenagers were this outspoken and smart. If so, no wonder so many parents grayed prematurely and ended up with ulcers. "So, are you saying we're driving you crazy?"

Lizzie ran across the room and grabbed Al into a bear hug. "Exactly! I love you both, but you're grown-ups. Don't you think it's time you act like it?"

"You know, Lizzie, some people might call your attitude impertinent," Al said with a wink.

"Yeah, maybe, but you know I'm right. I get my brains from my mom, and if she–" Lizzie paused, "if she were here, she'd be telling you the same thing."

Al reached up and touched Lizzie cheek. She brushed the single tear away and smiled. "She is here, and will be as long as you live. And for the record, you're both right. Maybe it is time we do something about this tension." Al took Lizzie by the hand and led her out the back door. "Sweetie, maybe you might wanna take a bike ride into town before dinner."

Lizzie stopped fast. "You aren't going to fight are you?"

Al laughed. "Not exactly. Don't worry, everything will be fine." Al marched across the street and followed Lizzie into the huge Victorian house. She stopped at the sound of Will's voice scolding Hoyden.

"Why don't you ever just play with your toys? You always have to ruin everything." He stormed out of the dining room carrying a half-chewed shoe. He glared at Lizzie when he spotted her. "I asked you to put her outside when I got in the shower."

"I forgot."

"Well, now I'm short a shoe. Thank you."

"I'm sorry. I'll replace it."

Will tossed the shoe into a pile of various other half-chewed items. "With what? Money I give you."

"Will!" Al had never seen him like this. The usually carefree man, who never stopped smiling, was all but foaming at the mouth. "Calm down."

"Oh wait, you have your own money. I forgot. No, actually I didn't forget. Your aunt won't let me. By the way, she called and left a message for you. Your check came to her house and she forwarded it here. She wanted to remind you not to let me cash the check. It is after all your money and not mine."

"You know she doesn't mean things when she says them." Lizzie's voice wavered and Al feared she might cry.

"Well, it's terribly kind of her to remind me every time she can. Maybe you could remind *her* that I don't steal your money."

"Whatever, Uncle Will. I'm going for a ride. I'll be back later."

"I don't think so, we have company for dinner."

"I know, but I'm suddenly not hungry."

Al gave her weak smile, a sort of apology on

Will's behalf, although heaven knows why she should defend his juvenile behavior.

"Don't go out that door, young lady," Will shouted at the door as it slammed shut. "Damn!"

"You expected something different?"

Will looked at Al. She stood in the foyer with her arms folded across her chest and her foot tapping on the hardwood floor. He remembered another night she'd done the same thing. A rush of *deja vu* swept through him, quickly replaced by a wave of guilt. "Why are you so early?" he snapped.

"I think a better question would be, what's wrong with you?"

His shoulders drooped and all the fight he had in him slipped out. He turned his back on her and walked to the living room. His fingers dug into the back of the loveseat and he leaned into it, the weight of his frustration pushing down. Frustration at himself for letting the old biddy get to him. What did he care what she thought of him?

"Will, what's this really about? I've never seen you like this before."

"Let's face it, Al, there's a lot about me you've never seen. You don't know me and you certainly don't know anything about my life."

His words stung more than they should have and Al considered walking away. She did more than consider it she turned and headed for the door. It wasn't her fault Grace had it in for him. Neither she nor Lizzie deserved his anger, and she for one didn't have to tolerate it.

"Maybe you know more than I give you credit for."

She stopped and considered his words. "What the hell is that supposed to mean?" Al spun around and glared across the room at his back. Somehow she sensed the change in topics. He was no longer talking about Grace. He was talking about their relationship. "No! You know what? I don't give a rat's–I don't care what you meant. Let me tell you something, buddy." She stomped across the room, arms swinging, and nostrils flaring. "You may think you know everything, but you don't know anything. I came over here tonight to tell you that I couldn't stop thinking about you and what happened between us." She clenched her fists at her sides, unwilling to give in to the urge to touch him.

He turned to face her. His eyes grew wide and his mouth dropped open.

"And furthermore, I have never wanted so much in my life to do the things to you that I want to do." She paused. "I only wish I knew what you wanted from me."

He turned his entire body around and moved toward her. There was no desire in his eyes, no longing in his expression, only sadness. "All I want from you is for you to hold me. Hold me in your arms like you hold me with those damnable eyes of yours."

"I don't know how to help you, but I know I want to." She wrapped her arms around him as he stumbled against her. His shoulders shook and his breathing became labored and raspy. She wondered if there were tears to go with the outpouring of emotions he showed her.

"They want to take Lizzie away from me."

"What?"

"They say I'm not fit enough to be her guardian, or anything to her for that matter. They say I'll never be able to give her the family environment she deserves."

Al brushed her cheek against his chest, wiping away the traces of tears from her own eyes. Lizzie belonged with Will and he needed her. They needed each other. She needed them. For years she'd feared never needing anyone and now that she did, she wouldn't give them up.

She didn't know how she knew it, but she knew she loved Will. More than anything she loved the man in her arms and she would do whatever necessary to make sure he had everything he needed, and right now, that meant Lizzie. All she needed now was a plan.

Allison stuffed the last bowl of strawberries into the basket before closing the lid. She patted the side of the wicker basket and wondered how all of this would affect Lizzie. Marriage was a serious matter, not something to be taken lightly. "So why am I about ask a man I barely know to marry me?" For nearly two weeks she'd spent time with Will and Lizzie. She'd done nothing but think about what she was about to do. "So, what do you think?" She looked down at Tippy who greedily chewed on the berry she'd tossed to her.

"Are you listening to me?"

The raccoon stopped and looked up at her. A stream of bright red berry juice dripped down her little gray chin. She twittered happily in her little critter voice before going back to his treat.

"Oh sure, everyone's full of advice." Allison reached down and scratched her soft tummy.

Always willing to accept affection, Tippy rolled onto her back and offered Allison better access to her stomach.

"Live it up, sweetie. Tomorrow it's back to the shelter with you."

With one last stroke, she pulled the basket of food off the counter and headed for the door. "You'll have to fend for yourself for a while. I've got some things to do."

Allison remembered the quilt she'd laid out upstairs, set the picnic basket on the floor, and scurried up the stairs.

She ran back down when the doorbell chimed. Her heart stopped for a brief moment when she opened the door and saw Will. She'd seen him every day for weeks and he still took her breath away.

"I got your message, Al. What's wrong?" He brushed past her into the house. "Are you all right?"

"I'm fine. I didn't mean to worry you. I have a problem and only you can solve it."

Will leaned against the wall and folded his arms over his chest. Allison watched the muscles in his forearms twitch as he drummed his fingers. "Must be important to leave such a cryptic message on my voice pager."

"Well, it is actually a matter of life and death."

He straightened up.

"Not like that though."

"Well, if you don't stop talking in circles my eyes are going to roll back in my head."

"Well how about you come with me and I'll explain everything."

She stood still as he circled her. She turned her head and met his gaze. Every inch of her body softened and she swayed on her feet.

"Well, since I'm here, I might as well."

"Good, then we should get going. I made a small lunch for us." She pointed down to the basket setting on the floor. "Would you mind?"

Will bent down and picked up the basket. "It feels like there's enough for an army."

"Not really."

Allison couldn't shake the case of nerves fluttering in her stomach as she drove to the lake. Several times she tried to start a conversation and finally turned on the radio. More than once she caught him staring at her, but neither spoke.

The sun hung low in the early evening sky as Allison parked the truck along the nature trail. She pulled the blanket out of the truck cab while Will grabbed the picnic basket. He held her elbow as they made their way down a slope to the edge of Gray Bear Lake.

They found a flat spot and worked together to spread the blanket out on the soft grass. Once they'd settled, Allison reached for the basket. Before she got her hand on the wicker top it flipped open and Stubby scurried out. The small hyperactive ferret scampered out of the box and onto Al's lap.

"What are you doing in there you little troublemaker?" The ferret stood on its hind legs and nuzzled her chin.

"I didn't know we were being chaperoned." Will peeked inside the basket. "Any more surprises in there?"

"I'm sorry about this." Allison pulled a corner of the blanket down and tucked the tiny creature under it.

Will laid out two plates and filled the two fluted glasses Allison had wrapped and tucked in the basket. Allison watched with amusement as Will glanced repeatedly toward the napping ferret.

"He won't bother us if we don't bother him."

His head snapped around and his cheek pinked. "I'm just not too comfortable with animals like this."

"Stubby is a baby. Technically he's full grown, but his accident has left him pretty timid."

Will leaned back on his elbow and stared at her. This time the heat of self-consciousness was in her cheeks. "Why are you staring at me?"

"It's the way you are with the animals. You're like *Dr. Doolittle* or something."

Allison tucked a grape into her mouth and considered his observation. She didn't really talk with them, but she understood their need to belong. Everyone deserved to belong someplace, even the animals. Her thoughts led her back to the reason for her picnic. "Will, I've been thinking."

"About?"

Allison fidgeted around on her corner of the blanket. She jerked back when her foot brushed against his thigh. "Would you do anything to keep Lizzie?"

"Sure, but I don't have a whole lot to offer." Will's voice shook and she almost lost her nerve. "I'd cut off my left arm, or whatever else."

"What if it meant doing something outrageous and even a little bizarre?" Al held her breath waiting for his answer.

"Al, is this something that could get us arrested?"

She giggled softly. "No, but it might get us committed."

"I think maybe you better just spill it."

Thirty minutes later, Will sat on the blanket cross-legged with his elbows resting on his knees and his head hanging down. He looked up at Al and shook his head. He stood up and paced the area around the blanket several times. "I can't ask you to do that."

"You didn't."

"Yeah, but under the circumstances, it isn't fair."

"I know life isn't always fair. Besides what would I lose?"

Will sat back down on the ground and rested his head in his hands. "Allison, this is absolutely nuts."

"Will, you've already said that about ten million

times. Get to the point before I start to believe you and have myself committed."

"I need to think about this. I'm not sure I'm ready to ruin someone else's life."

Without any further conversation, they gathered up their blanket and dishes and walked back to the truck.

They remained silent as they both entered Will's house. Will sat on one end of the sofa while Allison sat on the other.

The front door slammed open, then closed. Lizzie stepped into the doorway and looked at them. "Goodnight, Al." She turned and headed toward the stairs.

"Is she still mad at you?" Allison shook her head, *tsking* at him.

"Yeah, she's just like her mother when it comes to holding a grudge."

"Don't you think you should make up?"

"I guess I could make some kind of peace offering." Will smiled.

"Are you sure?"

Lizie stomped back into the room, but ignored Will.

"Lizzie, we need to talk." Will stood and moved toward the doorway. Lizzie kept walking. He looked to Allison for support. She shrugged and shooed him off. "Lizzie. Lizzie, stop." She made it to the top step before he lost it. "Fine, if you want to stay mad at me, great. No problem, your mom once stayed mad at me for two and half months. I'm tough, I can take it."

"Will, go after her," Allison commanded.

He spoke even as he moved toward the staircase. "I will not! If she wants to stay mad at me, fine, then she'll just miss the wedding."

Lizzie stopped walking and turned to face him.

"I don't suppose we need her there for it to be legal." He looked back at Al who was holding her head and rolling her eyes.

Lizzie stumbled down the stairs and Will turned back in time to catch her as she jumped into his arms from six steps up. "Oh, thank God!"

Will sat at the dining room table, Lizzie on one side, Katie on the other, and Al directly across from him. "But I don't want to wear a tuxedo."

"You have to. Al's dress is formal and you'll look stupid," Lizzie argued.

He looked at Katie. "So tell me again why the entire arch has to be covered with roses? Do you know how much that will cost?"

Allison sighed. "I still think we should just go downtown."

Will didn't like the glares coming from Katie and Lizzie. "I just think we're going overboard a little."

"I agree."

The girls continued to argue about wedding plans well into the night and for several more days. Allison spent every day with them, and he couldn't think of a single reason not to enjoy the rest of his life.

In two days time, Allison would be his wife. Everything else would come in time.

Allison stared at her reflection in the three-way mirror. The long satin gown cascaded out around her feet, the train of the dress covering a large portion of the bride's room floor. Small white flowers hung down around her face. The person staring back at her looked glowing and happy, not like her. She'd argued with Katie and Lizzie about going to the justice of the peace, but they'd insisted on a formal wedding. She didn't see the logic in it, but it meant a lot to Lizzie and that said everything. Nothing else mattered, only Lizzie.

"Al, are you sure you really want to do this?" Katie wrapped her arms around her shoulders and squeezed lightly. "There has to be another way."

"Oh please. You've planned this wedding to the hilt. You'd never forgive me if I didn't go through with it." Al smiled. Besides, if there were another way, they would have done it. Wouldn't they? It wasn't like this wedding would ruin anybody's life. It would help. Lizzie needed a good stable home life and she and Will could give it to her. It amazed her how much she'd come to love Lizzie in such a short time.

Here she stood in the back of a church; ready to marry a man she'd only known a short time, so she could be mother to a teenage girl. She'd lost her flea-pickin' mind. She did deserve to be committed.

A knock on the door startled her.

"Al, are you in there?" Will asked softly. Everyone in the room lunged when the doorknob turned.

"Will Hoyt, don't you dare come into this room." Katie slammed the door shut.

"Ouch, you shut my finger in the door." Will talked around the finger in his mouth. "I need to talk to Al."

"You'll have the rest of your life to do that, as soon as you're married."

Will sighed and pushed gently against the door. "This is important and it can't wait. I have to tell her something."

"Katie, let him in."

Will waited for the door to open, but it didn't. He leaned against it trying to make out the hushed words, but couldn't. "I mean it."

"I mean it, too," Katie snapped. "You are not coming in here and that's final."

"I need to warn her. Come on, Katie, this could be life or death." Will turned when he heard the heavy clicking of heels on the tile floor.

Grace stopped at the end of the hall and stared at him. He waited for the lightning bolts to follow his thoughts of blasphemy straight into his heart. This woman made him think things no good God-fearing man would dare.

"What is the problem here, Wilfred?"

How he hated it when she called him that. She did it just to irritate him and it worked very well. "Grace, I told you I would see if she had a minute. For cripe's sake, we're getting married in twenty minutes."

"Will, get away from the door and let me talk to her." Grace took the last few steps to the door and pushed him aside. "Allison, you don't know me, my name is Grace. I think we should speak before you do this."

Will listened to the flurry of activity behind the door. Then the door opened a crack.

"Will, get out of here, you still can't come in." Katie pushed against his shoulder. "Go on, we'll be fine.

"No, Katie, I think I need to stay." Nothing in the world could make him leave Grace alone with Al.

"Will, honey, go on and finish getting ready," Al said in her most charming southern drawl. "I want you looking like your usual dashing self when we meet at the altar. I can handle a few little minutes with Aunt Grace. Go on sweetie. Love you."

Except that. He could think of nothing in the world except the sound of those words rolling off Allison's tongue. The new sense of confidence in her blossomed inside him, and he knew she could handle Grace. "I'll see you in twenty minutes, darlin'."

"I'll be the one in too much white."

Will smiled as he walked away. For the first time in two weeks, he truly believed that this might be a good thing.

Allison met Grace's stare and held it. The woman was an Amazon. She stood at least a half a foot taller than her, and had the girth of a linebacker. To anyone else, she might have been intimidating, but Allison had principle on her side. She wasn't about to let this mammoth woman take Lizzie away.

"What can I do for you, Aunt Grace?"

"You can call me Grace." The tone of her voice did little to conceal her hostility.

"What is it you needed to say to me just before my wedding?" Al folded her arms across her chest.

"Could we have some privacy?"

"I think–" Katie started.

"It's all right, Katie. I'll be just fine. Wait outside; this will only take a minute."

Katie scooted everyone else out of the room and closed the door behind her.

Grace's eyes narrowed. "I know what you're doing, and it won't work."

"Well, as long as the minister is still ordained I think it will. We have everything we need to get married." Al enjoyed the sour expression on the old bat's face.

"Don't be flippant with me. I know you are only marrying that playboy because he thinks it will help him keep Lizzie."

"Will is a playboy? Oh my, I hadn't realized. I'm not sure if I want a carousing husband. That was the problem with the other four."

Grace's mouth dropped and her eyes bulged in their sockets. "You've been married four times already?" She began pacing the room. "What kind of example will that set for Lizzie? You're no better than him."

Al's patience snapped and she advanced on the woman. "That is where we agree on one thing. I'm no better than Will. I don't think anyone is. He is the most kind and considerate man I have ever met. He loves and adores Lizzie and he has done everything in his power to make a home for her."

"Oh please."

"No, you listen." Al jabbed her finger at the air between them. "You come into my wedding and you attempt to intimidate me to your way of thinking. Well, it won't work."

"You don't know what their family is like. That harlot sister of his turned my brother into an idiot. He lost sight of the values we'd been taught."

"You know, Aunt Grace, you have a lot of nerve standing in a church and speaking ill of the dead. Especially my family. In ten minutes you will have one more thing in your life to worry about."

"What's that?"

Al took another step and pulled herself up as far as she could to meet the huge woman's glare. "Me! Now get the hell out of this room and don't let me see you in that church or I'll have you thrown out on your–"

The door burst open. "Allison, it's time we get out to the sanctuary. I believe your groom is getting nervous, they've stapled his shoes to the floor at the front of the church, and he is straining against the chains." Katie turned to her husband. "Honey, would you see this person to her car? And then get your sweet handsome self up to the church so we can get these folks married."

Tony winked at Al and she blew him a kiss. When she was alone in the bride's room with Katie, she crumpled to the floor in a satin heap. Katie wrapped her arms around her and they rocked. They sat for a few minutes before Al gained some of her confidence back. Anger oozed from every pore and that alone kept her from crying and ruining the paint job Katie had worked so hard on.

"I think I could grow to hate that woman."

"Don't waste your energy, you're gonna need it for your wedding night." Katie chuckled.

"You are wicked." Al took Katie's hand and stood up. No one needed to know that there probably wouldn't be a wedding night. Only Al and Will knew that the wedding was a matter of convenience.

They smoothed out the folds in her dress and checked for spots and wrinkles. Once assured, they headed to the sanctuary.

◀ Eight ▶

Allison stood at the back of the church with her arm looped through Doc MacGruder's. He patted her hand and they started their walk.

"Your mamma would be so proud of you today. That Wilfred is a good man."

She swallowed past the lump in her throat and looked straight ahead.

Al never took her eyes off Will, who met her gaze. The minister said his piece and they answered in all the right spots. She tried to keep the excitement of her wedding day to a minimum, but Will standing beside her looking like sin wrapped with a bow, made it impossible.

"You may kiss your bride."

Will and Al stared at each other.

The minister's voice boomed a little louder the second time. "You may kiss your bride."

Allison turned her face toward the back of the church. Grace stood on the outside of the glass partition, her glare made Al think of a nuclear meltdown. She turned back to Will and smiled.

"Well, don't just stand there, kiss your wife," Katie urged.

Will lowered his head and covered her lips with his. Al put her arm around his neck and pulled him deeper into the kiss. Their tongues met in a moment of pure intimacy, the kind of intimacy a man and wife share for the first time. The knot in the pit of her stomach slowly unwound as they shared in the passion of something new and exciting.

"Somebody get a hose, quick before they burst into flames," Tony yelled.

Al lost the moment, when a laugh erupted between them. Will moved back, but only far enough for them to breathe. Their lips brushed together as they smiled. Al hoped the laughter and smiles would bode well for their marriage. No matter how convenient it was, she still would do everything in her power to make him and Lizzie happy.

The two of them stood at the back of the church greeting their guests and showing off their new matching wedding bands. The people of Brasselton warned Will about what would happen if he hurt their little Allie. He took the jibes in the manner in which they were intended, but didn't ignore the light tone of seriousness.

"Don't go hurtin' her or I'll have to get my book out on how to tie a good noose knot." The mayor's belly jiggled when he laughed at his own comment. Allison gave him a warm hug. With no family of her own, the town's support touched her. Then it dawned on her; she did have a family. She had a husband and a child to take care of.

She turned and watched Lizzie, who stood talking to Jamie Pickett. The two spent most of their time together and some maternal instinct told Al it was time to talk to Lizzie. How bizarre is that, she wondered. Me, with a maternal instinct.

"Should I go and break that little party up?" Will pointed toward Lizzie and Jamie. "I don't think I like him spending so much time hanging around."

"You'll leave them alone. If you'd like, I'll talk to her and make sure everything is okay." Panic streaked across his features and the color drained from his face. Al wondered if he might be about to faint. "Are you okay? What's wrong?"

"You tell me! What do you mean you'll make sure everything is okay? What could be wrong? You don't think she might be–why, I'll take him out and–"

Al laughed. She laughed so hard people turned and stared at her. Lizzie even stopped and glanced their direction. "I would think you'd have other things to worry about right now."

"Like what?" Will leaned down and whispered in her ear. "Should we slip off somewhere alone?"

Al turned his head and whispered back. "No, but we need to decide how to handle Grace." Not even ice-cold water could have doused his flame any faster. "Sorry, but she's on to you."

"I don't give a–"

"Will, we're in church."

He looked around, hoping none of the more mature guests, or, heaven forbid, the minister was anywhere near. "You never told me what happened when you talked."

"Please forgive me for being so inconsiderate. I had a few other things on my mind."

"What could be more important than that?" Will flinched when she punched him in the arm.

"You jerk!" Al pushed playfully against his arm. "I'm gonna tell my new husband you hurt my feelings."

Will opened his mouth to speak and then clamped it shut. "Oh, the wedding. I guess I for–well, I didn't actually forget, I just didn't think it–" he paused and took a deep breath. "I'm not having any kind of a wedding night after this, am I?"

"It's not looking too good for you, motor mouth."

Al gasped when he swept her into his arms and kissed her full on the mouth. Her arms snaked around his back and tugged him closer against her. Her heart raced as their tongues danced together. His hand moved along the bareness of her back and slipped closer down toward her–

"Hey, would somebody get these two a room?" someone yelled.

Will let her go. She clung to him for a moment to regain her balance before stepping back. "What was that all about?" Al asked.

"I was trying to make you forget that I was making a fool of myself and acting like a jerk." He gazed at her expectantly. "Did it work?"

Al raised a hand to her fluttering heart and smiled. "Well, there may be hope for you yet."

Neither noticed Katie standing next to them until she cleared her throat. "Would you two like to get on with the wedding festivities so you can be on your way?"

Will's hand slipped behind her and gave her bottom a quick pat. "I think that would be a good idea."

The reception hall was a burst of color. Red, to be more precise. Paper bells dangled from the ceiling in red and white. Red and black crepe paper hung twisted in arches across the room, dipping down to make a basket for the balloons. Allison looked around at the decorations and smiled. Lizzie had proclaimed herself in charge of that department and it looked as though she'd put her all into it. Black napkins with bright red rosebuds etched on the corner, sat elegantly at each place setting. Matching plates were set beautifully on each table and a buffet of food spread across several more tables. Candles glowed and cast shadows around the room.

"It looks like the devil himself exploded in here."

Al looked at Will and giggled. "Lizzie really outdid herself, huh?" Allison turned in time to see Lizzie barreling toward them.

"So, when are you two leaving?" She threw her arms around them and hugged them.

"Anxious to get rid of us, kiddo?" Will kissed her on the cheek.

"No–not really–I mean no."

Al and Will looked at each other and then back to

Lizzie. "What's up? Is there something we should know?" Al knew a set-up when she saw it. "I am starting to get worried."

"You should be; she is her mother's child." Will stopped and looked at Lizzie, he sighed a breath of release when the smile remained on her face.

"I'm okay, Uncle Will, mom would be happy if she could see this and since she can't I have to be happy enough for both of us."

Will cupped her cheek. "I love you, Lizzie."

"I know, Uncle Will. I love you, too."

Al stayed out of the exchange, reluctant to intrude on their moment. There would be plenty of time for Lizzie and her to grow closer. She wouldn't push her, or Will.

"I love you, too, Al."

A tear rolled down her cheek and Al hugged Lizzie tightly. "I couldn't love you more if you were my own."

"I am now. I always will be. Mom would be thrilled to know I'm going to have parents as great as her and dad."

"I know this is going to take some adjustments, but I really want you to know that you can come to me about anything." Allison brushed a hair back from Lizzie's face. "I know I'll never be able to replace your mother, and I wouldn't want to try, but I will always be here for you."

"I think I can handle loving you without forgetting them. They would really like you."

Nothing could have meant more to Allison than Lizzie's acceptance.

The three of them stood quiet for a moment before the music started and the crowd called for the bride and groom. Will swept his new bride out into the center of the room in a flurry of applause. He wrapped his arm around Allison and glided across the floor.

With each beat they grew more accustomed to the movement of each other's bodies. She fit so perfectly against him. Naturally. Her hand fit into his like they'd been molded together. Her curves fused against all of his grooves made him think of the night in the hammock. He remembered each moment they'd spent together.

How had they come to this point? It didn't matter. He knew he'd do anything to make her happy from this day on. He already had some ideas on how to win his new bride's heart. However, keeping it a secret wouldn't be easy, especially in Brasselton.

After several dances and the cutting of the cake, they made their exit. Birdseed flew through the air as they rushed toward the hideously painted car. Someone had spent a great deal of time attaching various articles, including beer cans, cowbells, and several helium filled condoms to the truck. Will stuffed his bride and her bulky dress into the cab and popped a condom with his key.

"Hey, that's one kid for sure if you need to use that one."

Will smiled at Tony as his wife smacked him for

his crudeness.

He jumped into the truck and drove off, waving at their friends as he headed toward home.

He'd made it to the middle of town before it occurred to them that they hadn't decided where to live.

He pulled the truck over onto the gravel.

"Will, what's wrong?"

"Where are we going?"

"We're going home. Where on earth do you think we're going?" Then she knew. They'd never discussed it. Where would they live? Would they actually cohabitate?

"I guess I assumed, but I never thought to ask. Since you've already given up so much for me, I guess we should move in with you. If that's okay?

"Touched by his willingness to please her, she reached over and touched his arms. She thrilled at the way his muscles twitched under her touch. "That's silly. There are two of you and it's not a big deal for me to move my stuff over."

"Are you sure?"

"Then there's Hoyden. You have a fenced yard and Lord knows we don't want that monster running wild, she'd destroy the town."

"Yeah, she's definitely a handful, like all the women in my life."

"I resent that remark," Al teased.

"I'll bet you do." He patted her hand and shifted the truck into gear. "It will only be temporary anyway.

The house is scheduled to be restored for the historic society."

"Then what are we going to do?"

"Well, I am in the construction business. I reckon I'll build us a house." He smiled.

"Well, we can talk about this later." Allison winked at him.

"I guess we can spend the rest of the weekend moving your stuff, at least the stuff you'll need right away."

"You think?"

Will pulled the truck into the driveway and hopped out. Hoyden barked a welcome from off in the distance. His heart raced as he helped Al out of the truck and they headed across the yard. Thunder clapped and a streak of lightning flashed across the sky. The first drops of an evening storm dropped onto the sleeve of Al's dress. She picked up her skirt and hurried toward the house, when out of nowhere Hoyden appeared.

With a yip, a bark, and no other warning, Al found herself flat on her back looking up into the same brown eyes that had started all of this.

"For cripe's sake, Hoyden." Will grabbed the dog by the collar and pulled her off Allison. "Are you okay, I don't know what it is about you that makes her do this."

Allison blinked away the raindrops that were now falling steadily into her eyes. The limp remains of her wedding curls stuck unceremoniously to her cheeks and her butt hurt. "Me either, but this puppy is on her way to obedience school."

Will sighed. "Been there, done that."

"Oh, then we'll just have to beat her," Allison mumbled.

"The line forms to the rear."

Allison sat up and looked over at the dripping dog and melted under the gaze of repentant chocolate brown eyes. "Oh fine, I won't beat you, but we're gonna have to talk about this welcome greeting you've grown so accustomed to inflicting on me."

Al smiled when Hoyden's tail wagged back and forth in the mud puddle forming under her bottom.

Will stepped forward and scooped Al up into his arms. Her breath caught and she considered struggling. "What are you doing?"

"Don't you know anything about weddings and romance and stuff? I'm carrying my bride over the threshold of her new home."

Al tried to wiggle free. "But I'm all muddy. You'll ruin your tux."

He got a firmer grip on her and kept walking. "Then it'll match your dress."

"Oh."

"Never let it be said I don't know about this stuff." Will made his way up the rest of the walkway and pushed the door open. As he entered the house he leaned to kiss her. Their lips were almost together when Hoyden pushed past him into the house. "No, Hoyden, don't get on the–"

Hoyden squished up onto the sofa and plopped down.

"Sofa." Al rested her head on his shoulder and they laughed. "If you put me down, I'll go and clean that up."

"Yeah, I know." He waggled his eyebrow at her.

"You'd rather the mud crust onto the material so the couch will be stained?"

He buried his face against her neck and breathed in. "I'll buy a new couch."

She sighed when his lips nibbled at her earlobe. "That's not practical."

"Yeah, I know. But quite honestly, I don't give damn about the couch right now."

His lips worked a trail down the side of her neck and stopped at her collarbone. A thrill swept through her, the sensation turning her thoughts inside out. With each breath she took, more of him penetrated her senses.

The smell of his cologne mixed with the sweet smell of Texas rain warmed her, while the dark glow of his eyes and the curve of his lips sent a chill up the length of her spine. The same chill exploded into an overwhelming need to get this man naked.

"Why are you looking at me like that, Al?"

The husky tone of his voice, the raspy breathing, and the trembling hands made her strong with the power only a woman possessed. A power so new to her. Everything about him made her weak and yet strong at the same time.

She'd wondered what would happen when they got home. Their time together had brought them closer and she enjoyed the teasing moments they'd shared. As much as he'd joked about it, the idea of intimacy had not been discussed. Her insides warmed at his obvious intent.

Without putting her down, he moved toward the stairs. A memory of their first time took her breath away. He paused at the bottom and looked at her, a knowing twinkle in his eye.

"Not this time. This is your wedding night and it will be something worth remembering."

She reached out and stroked his cheek. "I'll always remember that night. I learned something about myself because of you."

"We both learned something then."

"What did you learn?"

"I learned that you drive me wild and that of we don't stop talking and move, I'm gonna ruin all my own plans."

Will set her down in the center of his bedroom. When he finally looked around, he noticed several things out of place. Well, not really out place, more like in place. He picked up a book of matches and lit several of the candles someone had set around the room.

The soft scent of vanilla, mixed with cinnamon, wafted around them, normal, and yet exotic. Will stepped up in front of her and touched the tip of his finger to her jaw. His hand slipped down to rest on her shoulder.

Standing there looking at her, it all became crystal clear. He looked into the eyes of the most beautiful woman alive, his wife. It could be forever or long enough to ensure he didn't lose Lizzie. How long did he want it?

"Does it feel very weird to you?" Her soft red lips moved in a way that made him want to devour her. She stared up at him and ran her tongue across her lower lip.

Will reached up and his finger followed the trail her tongue had taken. Her eyes closed. He leaned forward and kissed one lid, then the other. His breath caught when she sighed and her breath skimmed softly across his chin. He reached behind her and fumbled with the loops on her dress.

Frustrated with his trembling hands, he turned her around so he could see what he was doing. Kneeling down, he kissed the bare spot after each button came free.

Inch by inch her dress fell open.

He pressed his lips to her bare back and reveled in the way she leaned back into him. His hands pushed the dress apart and it slipped down to the floor around her ankles. She turned and stepped out of the folds of fabric.

Will stood and swept her into his arms.

When she turned into him and took his mouth with hers, something primal and instinctive snapped inside her. Her hands plunged into his hair and she pulled him against her, hungry for the sweet taste of his mouth.

After several long kisses, she broke away and smothered his face and neck with more unhurried kisses. Each one being met with another sigh from him. She groaned as they fell to the bed and his body covered hers.

"You're dressed and I'm naked."

He could barely find his breath to speak. "Not entirely naked." His hands rested on her thigh and unhooked the garter holding her stocking up. Little by little he rolled the nylon down until it slipped off her foot.

His lips kissed the tip of each of her toes. He moved back up and did the same with her other leg.

Allison sat up and pulled him between her legs. As quickly as her hands could move, she took his clothes off. Nothing erotic or passionate. Lust. Simple need drove her to get him naked as fast as she could. When he finally stood before her wearing nothing but a lazy smile, she pulled him back down on top of her.

"I want it to be slow and passionate, Al. I want it to be special." He struggled to pull away from her, enough to gain control, but she wouldn't allow it.

"It will be, next time."

His eyes rolled closed and his mouth dropped open.

The hair on his chest brushed against her nipples and she gasped against the sensation. A coarse layer of stubble scratched her cheek and she sighed with longing. Will pressed against her, and she arched toward him.

Allowing him access to her opened a new door of feelings she didn't think she could live through. Her stomach tightened as he drove himself deeper inside her. Bliss didn't begin to describe the sensation of their bodies adjusting to one another in the most intimate way.

They kissed, tongue pushing against tongue, hands touching and pinching. Will moaned out loud when she raked her fingernails down his back. Allison pushed her hips against him. She needed more. She needed him deeper.

In one swift motion, she shoved him back. He rolled to his side and she followed, ending up straddling his waist.

With as much enthusiasm as she'd ever had, Allison rode her husband. He bucked against her, his fingers digging into her hips as she writhed and rocked. The soft folds of her body teased him as she leaned forward and brushed her hair across his stomach.

The muscles in her thighs trembled as she clung to him, riding the waves of each stroke and thrust.

"Will, I want you so much," she mumbled against his shoulder.

He felt her words more than he heard them, but it was all he needed to reach the point of no return. He rolled her back underneath him and drove as deep as he could. Every ounce of life, his existence, exploded, pouring into her. She clutched at his shoulders and wrapped her legs around his thighs as they climaxed together.

Warmth flooded through his entire body, with frightening intensity. Afraid he would open his eyes and find it all to be a dream, he clung to her. They both trembled.

He slipped his arms under her and rolled onto his back, pulling her on top of him. In a tangle of damp sheets and sweaty limbs, they lay in each other's arms, gasping for air.

Will kissed the top of her head and she found the strength to open her eyes. She looked up to find him staring down at her. The smoldering look still in his eyes led to several more hours of lovemaking unlike she'd ever known. When she finally closed her eyes to sleep, the first rays of the morning sun were peeking in through the pale blue blinds.

The bleeping of a phone, somewhere in the house disturbed her dream. She'd had the most wonderful dream about getting married and falling asleep in her new husband's arms.

The smell of fresh coffee forced her to open her eyes. When she tried to sit up everything came rushing back. Will lay next to her, technically across her. One arm flung over her chest and his leg looped around hers. "Oh my." If he were in bed with her, who was making coffee?

"Morning, Al. I can't believe you already got up and made coffee."

"I didn't."

They both sat. A split second later they heard a light thud and feet scuffling down the hall. Will, unashamed and completely at ease with his nudity, crawled out of bed and pulled open the door. A tray filled with fresh croissants, honey butter, scrambled eggs, bacon, ham, and various types of fresh fruit lay on the floor at her feet. Two white roses stood in a bud vase with a note card leaning against it.

Thought you might have worked up an appetite.
Love, Katie and Tony.

Most of the morning passed before the newlyweds left the bedroom. The breakfast tray sat on the floor half empty and the sheets hung off the edge of the bed. Will crept down the steps in his boxers, Allison trailing close behind him. When no one popped out of the closets, or appeared in any of the rooms, they scampered into the kitchen. They laughed and joked as they worked side by side to prepare a light, cool lunch.

"This is kinda weird. Don't you think, Al?"

"That depends on what you are talking about." Al leaned back in her chair and propped her feet up on the edge of the table.

"Well, we could start with that." Will pointed to her feet.

She quickly pulled her feet down. Her first day in her new home and she'd already messed up. Living with someone would take some getting used to. At home–in her home–across the street, she could put her feet wherever she darn well pleased.

The phone in the kitchen bleeped its presence and Will scowled. "Don't they know we're on our honeymoon?"

Allison laughed. "Evidently not." Al stood up and reached for the phone. "May I?"

"Hey, you're the wife, it's your job to do all that kind of stuff now." Will ducked away from the towel flying at his head. "I guess not."

◀ Nine ▶

Al recognized Grace's sharp and irritatingly whiny voice after the first words. "Where is my niece?"

"Well, good morning to you too, Aunt Grace." Al motioned for Will to sit back down when he bolted out of his chair. She punched the speakerphone button and set the receiver back down. "What can I do for you this morning?"

Grace's voice blared across the kitchen. Al noticed the lines forming across Will's forehead and wished she'd handled the old busy body herself. "I want to know what you've done with Lizzie, while you two are playing your little sex games."

"Are there supposed to be games? I could have sworn they told me that marriage was serious and not a game."

A brief pause echoed the tension on the other end before Grace started in again. "You think you're a clever girl, but you'll see when you get your heart broken by another of those damn Hoyts. They're nothing but trouble and you'll do good to get out while you can."

"Aunt Grace, what exactly is it you called to say?" Allison held up a finger to shush Will when his mouth opened. "I have a lot to do today, and I quite honestly don't have time for your ranting and raving about nonsense."

"I called to talk to Lizzie. I have that right, you know."

"Yes, of course you do. I would never suggest you didn't. I'll be sure and give her the message that you called when she gets home."

"Where is she?" The voice on the other end went up an octave and the phone protested with a blast of static. "What have you done with her?"

"Grace, it is none of your concern where Lizzie is. We are her guardians, and you'll do good to remember that. Now, if you'd like to set up a time to come to our home to visit with her, please call anytime. Otherwise, I have things to do and my husband is waiting for me."

Allison hit the button and the phone disconnected. She picked her cup up off the table and took a sip. Or tried to. Her hand shook so badly she nearly drowned in sloshing coffee. She tried to steady the cup with her other hand. Will moved next to her before she could say anything. He took the cup out of her hand and held them between his.

"Why didn't you let me talk to her? She has no right to say those things."

"I thought it was my job to handle those kinds of things." Allison tried to force a laugh, but only succeeded in snorting. "I knew what it would be like when I suggested this, and I am not going to let her rule our lives."

"God, Al, do you always have to be so strong?" He wrapped his arms around her and pulled her against his chest.

"Yes." A deep rumble in his chest eased the tension tying her insides into knots. Slowly, she let herself relax and thanked the strength of her new husband.

The bleeping of the telephone interrupted them again. This time Will snatched it up off the hook. "This better be good."

Al watched his expression brighten. The soft lines across his forehead smoothed out and a dimple in his left cheek replaced them. A smile spread across his face and lit up his eyes. Al wondered how she'd managed to get such a handsome husband. Too many things about him made her heart race.

"Well, I guess that'd be okay. When will you be home? Okay. Love you too, kiddo." Will hung up the phone.

"Was that Lizzie? Or was it your other girlfriend?"

"You're in luck, it was Lizzie. She wanted to know if she could go with Katie and Tony, to his folks' lake house."

Allison's heart skipped a beat. Nerves had her hoping Lizzie would come home and give her an excuse to figure out what she'd done. She needed to figure out how she would keep Will interested in her, once the novelty of being married would die down, and surely it would. How long could they play the happy couple? It was time to start figuring out what they had to do to become Lizzie's legal parents.

She looked at the smile on her new husband's face and reminded herself, theirs was a marriage of convenience, and great sex was just an added bonus.

He dipped his head and nuzzled his lips against her neck. "Looks like it's just the two of us for the next three days." His hands splayed across her bottom and lifted her up onto the counter.

Small shivers of excitement raced along her nerves and she let herself get lost in the sensations of his mouth teasing her feverish skin. How could she think when his tongue laved at her ear and then her neck? Pin prickles of pleasure danced along her spine and finally she gave in to the tenderness of his touch. Her back arched and she slipped into the rhythm of his passion. His lips brushed against hers and she clung to him, enjoying the swirling of her senses.

By late afternoon they lay on the couch, one on each end, their legs tangled together. Hoyden lay on the floor next to them, catching the grapes that didn't make it into their mouths.

Allison tried not to think about the chore ahead of her. She decided to move her clothes first then worry about the rest later.

Part of her feared getting too comfortable in a situation that might only be temporary. She had no idea how long her marriage to Will Hoyt would last, or if it would.

"I think we need to get some of your stuff over

here," Will said quietly. "I'll make room in my closet for your clothes."

"I thought I would just bring over a few things for now." His frown caught her by surprise and she didn't hide it well. "What's wrong?"

"I'm not sure, but I get the feeling something's bothering you."

"No, not really. I just don't want to come in and take over your space."

Will pulled his legs back and sat on the edge of the couch. He'd suspected she had some qualms about their marriage, but he'd hoped she would see that it was more than convenient to him. "So, exactly how long are you planning on staying?" The sarcasm in his voice surprised even him. "You'll at least give me time to get full custody before you leave."

Her eyes glazed over with tears and he wished he could take back his words. She gathered her legs up against her chest and stared off across the room. He hadn't meant to make her cry, but why couldn't she admit there was something between them? Something other than convenience. "Allison, I didn't mean it to come out like that."

She bounced off the couch and turned her back on him. "I'll stay as long as you need me." Then she walked away.

Well, at least he wasn't in fear of losing her any time soon. He'd never needed anyone the way he needed her, but he knew she spoke of a different kind of need. He'd just have to make her understand. The front door slammed shut and he knew it wouldn't be easy.

Life had done quite a number on his new bride's self-esteem and he had no idea how to fix it. He'd never loved anyone who didn't want to be loved.

Instead of going after her, he moved his clothes to one side of the walk-in closet. He emptied half the dresser and fought with himself about throwing away some of his more *comfortable* clothes. Unable to toss them, he opted for packing them away. He finished taping up the last box as Allison walked in the front door. He shoved the box against the wall and sat back on his heels. She stopped inside the front door when she saw him.

"I have a few boxes ready to come over. Would you help me carry them?"

Her eyes were rimmed-red and he knew she'd been crying. The idea that he'd made her cry ate at his insides. "Al, I'm really sorry–"

"It'll be dark soon; we should get them over here." Allison turned to walk away then stopped. "Thanks for coming after me," she whispered. Would it have been so hard for him to care about her feelings?

"I thought–"

"Forget it, Will."

"Okay." He stood and followed her out the door. As she walked down the steps, he reached for her hand, only to have her pull away and pick up her pace. The pain of rejection soared through him and he sulked along behind her.

Two trips later, they'd moved everything she had packed. No personal items, only clothes. Systematically, she put them into the places he'd cleared. She neither looked at, nor spoke to him as she emptied the boxes. When the last box sat empty in the middle of the room, she headed for the door.

"I think that's enough for tonight. We can get the rest tomorrow."

"I can't."

"Why not?"

Allison turned and faced him. "I have to go to work. I need to start looking for shelters to move the animals to. They're about to be homeless."

Her barb hit its mark, cutting swift and deep and he acknowledged one more obstacle he'd have to overcome. He'd told her about buying the land, but after his week of working with her, neither of them had brought it up again. He'd already begun amending his plans for what to do with the land, but he hadn't thought to tell her about them. With the wedding and everything, there hadn't been a good time. Now seemed like the perfect time.

"Al, I think we need to talk about the shelter."

"A deal is a deal. You agreed to work for a week and you did. Since you didn't mention changing your mind, I assume you haven't. Katie and I are going to organize a bazaar to help get some of the animals adopted or at least get some money to move them to new shelters."

"That's what we need to talk about." Will tried to

say his piece, but she'd have no part of it.

"Don't worry; I won't make a big deal about it. This is something I have to do. I don't expect you to understand how important this is to me."

What exactly did she take him for? From the way she made it sound he'd enjoy seeing the animals booted out into the wilderness. For cripe's sake, he'd almost grown to like the pesky little animals, but she hadn't bothered to even ask what he thought about the situation. This is where they'd started. Maybe it was time he taught her a good lesson about assumptions and where they lead.

Lizzie picked up the phone and dialed her aunt's number. She clicked her nails on the kitchen counter while waiting for someone to pick up. The machine clicked on and Lizzie waited for the beep. "Aunt Grace, it's Lizzie. I wanted to let you know that I got your message and I'll be home in a couple of days."

"Lizzie, is that you? Where on earth are you?"

Her aunt's voice screeched through the line and snapped the quiet around Lizzie. She knew the panicked tone and wished she'd give Uncle Will a chance. Didn't she understand how everything was changing? Allison made Will smile. She made everyone smile. She was the first person to treat her like an adult, and she had to be the most loving person she'd ever met, except her mom.

"I'm at the lake with Katie and Tony. Don't worry about me, I'm staying here a while."

Grace's voice went up to the point of yelling. "I knew it. He married that silly woman and then dumped you off on someone else." She paused and took several deep breaths. "Tell me where you are and I'll come and get you."

"No. Stop it, Aunt Grace. I haven't been dumped off. Uncle Will and Allison are on their honeymoon." For the first time, Lizzie understood some of her uncle's frustration. Why couldn't she just understand?

"Lizzie, tell me where you are. You don't need to make excuses for them. I don't blame you for trying to cover up for him."

Lizzie heaved a deep breath. She looked at Katie, who stood across the room, and rolled her eyes. "I'm fine. I wanted to come to the lake. I like Katie and Tony."

"Tony? That horrible man who threw me out of the wedding. Imagine, me not being welcome."

"Well, you did come and make a scene. How could you do that?" Lizzie let some of her anger spark. "You don't think he's good enough to take care of me, and you make sure everyone knows how much you don't like him."

"Liz, honey. I don't want you to be upset by any of this. They only got married because they think it will stop me from getting custody of you. They don't love each other and are probably not capable of loving you or anyone else."

Lizzie let the phone drop down against her shoulder. Could it be true?

"Lizzie, are you there?"

Swallowing past the lump in her throat Lizzie tried to make sense of the past few weeks. Uncle Will was happy. Wasn't he? "I'm here."

"Think about it, Honey. Do people really *fall in love* overnight? I know you are smart enough to understand the implications of this. Their marriage is convenient for now, but what about later?"

Had she become such a pain for her uncle that he'd been forced to get married? How could that be? Allison loved them. Didn't she? "Don't worry about me. I know perfectly well what's going on. I have to go, Aunt Grace."

"You just hold on, Lizzie and I'll get you back very soon."

Lizzie held the phone, but felt nothing.

"Honey, what's wrong?" Katie slipped into the chair next to Lizzie. "You look like you just lost your best friend."

"I think I did." She made her way to the table and tried to ignore the soft voice in the back of her head. Couldn't anyone be honest? Did they always have to think they were protecting?

"Tell me what's wrong. Maybe I can help."

Lizzie stared down at the table and tried not to cry. How could her Uncle and Al have lied to her like this? She needed them, but more than that she needed them to be honest with her.

"Honey, tell me."

Lizzie lost the battle against her tears and they

streamed down her cheeks. Without thought she fell into Katie's arms and sobbed. Her heart ached as she thought of her uncle giving up his freedom and his prized bachelor status to give her a place to live. "I need to go to my Aunt Grace's house."

"What on earth for, Lizzie?"

"I can't let them do this. I know why they got married and I can't let them give up their lives like this. Not for me." Lizzie jumped up and ran out of the room.

Katie turned to her husband who had walked into the room in time to hear her tear-filled confession. "What on earth was that all about?"

"I wish I knew Tony. I wish I knew."

He picked the phone up off its cradle and handed to her. "Well, you need to call the lovebirds and let them know that all hell just broke loose and to get dressed."

Will rolled off the couch and grabbed the phone up. "Slow down, Katie. I can't understand what you're saying."

Al came into the room and grabbed the handset from him. "Katie what is it? Is Justin all right?" She dropped down onto the couch and Will tried to grab the phone back, but she wouldn't let go. "No, I'll be right there."

She hung up and grabbed her shoes off the floor.

"Where do you think you're going? And what was that all about?"

"I have to go get Lizzie." She pulled away from him, but he followed her upstairs. What had she been thinking to marry a man she barely knew? "This is all my fault. Please let me do this."

He stopped short of grabbing her and she turned to face him. "Have you forgotten that she is my–"

She glared at him. "Don't you dare try to leave me out of this."

"*Our* responsibility?" Will amended.

"That's not what you said."

"It's just that I've known Lizzie all her life and I understand how she feels. I think it will be better if we show a united front."

"No Will, you don't understand. That's why I need to go to her." She took his hand in hers. "Katie says she feels like you betrayed her and I have to go and explain that it was me not you."

"But it wasn't, Al." He pulled her closer and lifter her chin up. "We made a decision together and it was the right decision. I think we need to do this together so Lizzie understands that we haven't betrayed her."

Will pulled on a pair of jeans and they headed to the lake together. They arrived to find Lizzie sitting on the front porch step with her overnight bag setting next to her.

"What's up, kiddo?" Al stepped toward her, but Lizzie turned away.

"Lizzie, what's going on? What's all the fuss?"

Lizzie stood and shoved her bag off the step. "Leave me alone."

"I don't think I can do that. It seems as though you're stuck with me for a very long time." Will leaned toward her and reached out to touch her cheek. His finger brushed up against the warm tear rolling down her face. His stomach knotted and his own eyes filled with tears.

"Stuck with you? Don't you mean you're stuck with me?" Lizzie headed off down a path leading to the lake.

"Lizzie, wait." Al chased after her and Will brought up the rear.

He struggled to keep up with the women in his life, but they rounded a curve and he had to double his steps to get them back in his sights.

"What are you talking about? Nobody is stuck with anybody. We're a family. That's what this is all about."

Will listened as Allison tried to console a weeping Lizzie.

"Sweetheart, we love you. I thought you knew that."

Lizzie's sandal clad feet slapped against the boards of the rickety dock and Will finally caught up. He had to get in shape if life with women was going to be like this.

"You don't love me–well, you might love me, but you don't love each other. How can we be a family if you don't even love each other?"

Will stared at Al and had no idea what to do. "Honey, I don't understand why you would think that."

"What's to understand, Will?" Lizzie started to turn away from them. "You don't love each other."

He cringed at the impersonal use of his name. "Please, Lizzie."

"No, Will, let her speak her mind." Al took his hand and squeezed it. He needed the support. For a brief moment, he wondered if Grace hadn't been right. Maybe he couldn't take care of Lizzie.

"When you said you were getting married I was so excited. I didn't think I'd ever be as happy as I was–" she gulped before going on, "–when mom and dad were alive."

"That's what we want. We want you to be happy." Al reached for her and she didn't pull away. "We would never do anything to hurt you and we would never do anything to hurt ourselves."

"You only accepted his proposal to keep Aunt Grace from taking me away."

Will stepped forward and opened his mouth to speak, but Lizzie cut him off. "Why would you do that?"

"First of all, Lizzie, I didn't accept your uncle's proposal. I asked him to marry me."

Lizzie stopped and looked from one of them to the other.

"I knew the moment I saw him that there was something about him."

"You did?" Will and Lizzie asked at the same time.

Allison turned and faced the water, her back to

them. "It was your uncle's big brown eyes that floored me. How could anyone resist them?"

Heat rushed into Will's cheeks and he stepped toward her. "I'm glad you couldn't." Lizzie touched Al's shoulder and Will waited.

A small speedboat whizzed across the lake and set about a pattern of waves. The water slapped against the pylons holding the dock up. The force of the water rocked the walkway gently. Lizzie paced a small path across the dock as she contemplated the conversation.

She folded and unfolded her arms before stopping to face them both. "I don't know what to think." She walked toward the end of the dock and Will jumped in front of her.

"Lizzie, I don't do anything I don't want to. Unless Katie bullies me into it." Al grinned.

"But what about what Aunt Grace said."

"What did she say? And how in the hell would she know?" Will snapped.

"Will, stop it."

"I don't know, but when I talked to her she said that you two didn't want to get married. She told me you only did it so she couldn't take me away." Lizzie stepped forward and Will backed up, giving her space.

"I would do anything to keep you with me, kiddo." Lizzie started walking again and Will carefully stepped backward in front of her. "I love you."

"And I love you, but I couldn't bear it if I thought you had given up your freedom for me. Either of you."

"Lizzie, I can't think of anywhere I would rather

be than with you and your uncle. And that has everything to do with love, not legalities."

Will kept back-stepping as the two women rambled on.

"Um, Uncle Will–"

His heart skipped with joy when she called him uncle. Maybe they could salvage things if he could only get his–

Al doubled over and swiped the tears of laughter off her cheeks. She grabbed Lizzie's hand as they peered over the edge of the dock at Will floundering in the water. He looked cute as a button with his blond hair dripping water into his eyes. He'd looked nearly the same the first time she'd seen him with rainwater dripping out of his hat and down his face. He slapped at the water and cursed under his breath.

"Honey, you need a hand?" Al giggled.

"That's not funny. Could you pull me up, please?"

Al and Lizzie looked at each and nodded their agreement. They turned and walked away, leaving Will to paddle in the rippling lake.

"Come on you two. You can't make me swim all the way to shore."

They stopped and giggled again before turning around and walking back to the end of the dock. At the same time they leaned forward and each offered a hand to pull him up. Al should have seen it coming, but the smoldering look in his deep brown eyes sucked the good sense clean out of her. Before they could let go,

Will set a foot up against a beam and yanked them both into the water.

"You think that's funny, do ya?" Will splashed water toward both of them as they all wrestled around in the frigid lake.

Al enjoyed the carefree frolicking between them and prayed it would last. This situation was inevitably the first of many hurdles they'd have to jump.

When she noticed Lizzie's lips turning blue, she suggested they head toward the shore. Katie waited on the beach with three fluffy warm towels. She gently squeezed Lizzie and Al's shoulders before silently walking away.

The three of them sat down on the plastic lawn furniture and stared at each other for several awkward moments. Al's heart wept for both of the people next to her whom she had grown to love. She would do anything to take away the hurt and insecurities she saw in both their faces.

Finally, Will broke the silence. "Lizzie, you have to believe that we love you and would do anything in our power to make you happy. But we would never hurt you."

"I know that. It's just that–"

"I'm not saying this because of my feelings for her, but you cannot believe everything that your Aunt Grace says." Will pleaded with his eyes and Al watched Lizzie's demeanor soften.

"But you two hardly know each other. It makes sense that you would do this just to protect me."

Al couldn't stay out of it any longer. "I'll say it again. I don't do anything I don't want to do and there are any number of other ways we could have protected you." Will's head snapped up and he stared at her.

"Exactly. The way Al and I feel about each other has nothing to do with you or anyone else. We are grownups."

Al thanked the gods for the twinkle in Lizzie's eyes.

"Well, Uncle Will, sometimes you sure don't act like it."

Will chuckled and the sound of laughter warmed her. "It's getting cold out here and if we don't get out of these wet clothes, we're all going to end up sick." Al stood and held out her hand for Lizzie. The teenager gave it a squeeze then tucked it into her uncle's larger hand.

"I love you both." And off she ran.

"She's a wonderful kid." Will stared after her, a tear resting at the corner of his eye. "I don't know what I would do if I ever lost her."

"Well, then I suggest we don't let it happen."

He looked down at her and she thought her insides might melt. How could she go on living in a marriage with a man she loved hopelessly? Especially when she didn't have the nerve to tell him.

◀ Ten ▶

Al rolled over on her side and snatched another Kleenex off the bedside table. The soft tissue against her nose tormented her yet again. She had no idea how many times she'd blown her nose in the last twenty-four hours. She flipped back over and glared at Will, who lay sleeping soundly beside her.

The annoying buzz of his snoring set her frazzled nerves on edge. She knocked her elbow against his pillow. He sniffled several times, rolled over onto his other side, and returned to slumberland. How did he do that? She'd taken every imaginable cold remedy, the same as him, but she lay awake. The creaking of the door pulled her attention away from her husband.

"Ah, you're awake," Lizzie beamed. "I waited to come up so you could get some rest."

Al sighed. "The only one here getting any rest is Rip Van Winkle." The smile on Lizzie's face did more to make her feel better than all the medicines put together.

"Uncle Will could sleep through a hurricane if it blew him out of bed." Lizzie poked the bottom of his foot poking from under the blanket.

He kicked at the irritation, coughed, and slept on.

"I think I hate him," Al coughed.

A flash of concern washed over Lizzie's face and Al grabbed her hand. "I'll love him again when I'm not sick and he's still miserable."

"I feel so bad about all this." Lizzie set a tray of steaming broth on the bedside table and climbed in next to Allison.

"Why should you feel bad?" Allison leaned back and elbowed Will again. "I'm blaming old Buzz here. No one else."

"Seriously Al. I should have trusted you both to be honest with me."

"Oh sweetie, you know we would never do anything–"

"I know. I'm fine now. I just wish the two of you felt better. So much is going on and I just don't know what to do."

Allison wrapped an arm around her and nudged Will with her hip. He grumbled and snuggled up against her, tossing an arm over her legs.

"He does that all the time. Sometimes I feel like I'm suffocating."

Lizzie laughed. She lifted his arm and let it drop. "It would be cute if he wasn't such an oaf."

The teenager's infectious laugh lifted her drooping spirits and offered a ray of hope for survival. "So tell me what's been happening. I hate that you've been fending for yourself for the last few days."

"I'm fine. I learned how to cook a long time ago and I'm grown now, so I can do most anything myself."

"Did Katie call?"

"Yeah. She said everything is fine at the shelter and if you ask me, she's having a ball being back there."

"I know she misses it." Al sneezed. "Are you sure you're doing okay?"

"Yes, *Mother*," Lizzie sighed dramatically.

Her heart skipped a beat or two and Allison hugged her closer. Wouldn't that be nice? It warmed her to think of being someone's mother some day. "I know. Soon you won't need us anymore and then what will we do?"

Lizzie hugged her. "Oh I'll always need you. Both of you."

"What's a man have to do to get some shut eye around here?" Will tugged at Al's legs and pulled her tighter against him.

"Oh please. Who could sleep with all the snoring?"

"Don't worry, your snoring didn't bother me in the least." He rubbed his eyes and rolled over to stretch himself across the bed. "Are we having a party?"

Al sneezed and Lizzie dropped off the edge of the bed. Her laugh and loud thump brought Hoyden running full tilt into the bedroom. Before anyone could stop her, the retriever barreled up onto the bed and sent Allison full force against the headboard.

"Sheesh. Why is this beast always jumping on top of me?"

They all laughed while Will and Lizzie tugged at

the dog's collar, trying to get her off the bed.

Three days later they were again tugging Hoyden off the bed. "Come on you beast. I just want to make the stupid thing. It's what wives do." Allison tugged while Lizzie pushed.

"Well, if it isn't my three favorite women." Will leaned causally against the frame of the bedroom door looking gloriously handsome in his jeans and shirt.

"You could help." Allison tossed a pillow at him and Hoyden flew after it.

He threw it back and before she knew it, they were all rolling around on the bed tugging at the dog and getting tangled in the sheets and blankets.

"Do any of you know how much it costs me emotionally to make a bed? For the love of Mike." Al yanked on the sheet and Will rolled toward her.

He pulled her into his arms and up against his chest. "Hey, who is this Mike guy and what's he doing with my wife?" He kissed her nose and she pushed him away.

"Oh grow up," Al teased. "This is the new Millennium and stuff like this happens all the time."

His eyes twinkled and his mouth crooked up in a playful smile. "Not in my marriage it doesn't. I'm all the man you can handle."

"Yuck. I think this is my cue to get out. I've got to go call Jamie. A bunch of us are going to the movies in town later and I need to tell him what time to pick me up."

Before he could argue Al waved Lizzie away.

"Wait a minute. I don't remember anyone asking me if this was okay." Will sat up.

"I told her it was all right. There are several going and one of the girl's parent's is going to drive them both ways."

Allison wanted to reach out and brush the worry from his expression, but something stopped her.

"So what are we supposed to do?"

Al smiled. "We could always watch a movie at home."

He turned to face her completely and took her hands in his. "Or we could move the rest of your things over. Its time we make this official."

She climbed off the bed and paced the room.

Will watched her go back and forth. How could he make her understand that he wanted her with him always? He'd waited for the perfect time to tell her how much he truly loved her, but it never came.

"I think things are going pretty well."

"I agree. That's why I want to make things right. Lizzie asked why you hadn't moved your stuff over."

She stopped and stared at him. "What did you tell her?"

The soft glow in her eyes worried him. If an outsider looked into them they would think she was happy, but he knew better. He'd learned to read her expressions and right now something was going on in her head. Something he needed to know about and fix.

"I told her we weren't sure what you were keeping.

I explained that it would take time."

"Time. Everything takes time."

He went to her and swept her into his arms. At first she pushed against him, but he refused to let her go. Finally, she wrapped her arms around his waist and they stood together. He held his wife in his arms and wished with all his heart he could make her happy.

Life had really done a number on both of them and he had no clue how to make it right.

"I'll be fine. Let's go get my stuff."

The next three weeks passed without incident and Will couldn't have been more pleased. Lizzie had returned to her normal teenage self and Al had kept busy with the multi-legged hooligans she called pets at the shelter. They ate together as a family every night and they settled in to a nice lifestyle.

Until the bottom fell out on a perfectly good Friday evening.

Will leaned over to flip the burgers on the grill when Lizzie came tearing into the back yard. "I was nominated to be homecoming queen."

Will stopped cold.

"Lizzie, honey, that's wonderful." Al stood and hugged her. "I'm so happy for you."

"Wonderful? Happy? Are you crazy?" Lizzie cried.

Will plopped down onto the picnic bench. "Here it comes."

"This is horrible. I'll be ruined. Everything will be

ruined."

"My life is over and I'll never be able to show my face again." Will mimicked Lizzie as she lamented the many woes of her life. He'd heard it all before.

He stopped when Al's foot landed squarely against his shin.

"Ouch, why'd you do that?" He leaned forward and rubbed the tender spot.

"You are not helping things one bit."

"He doesn't care. He only cares about his stupid business." Lizzie fell into Al's welcoming arms.

Will considered kicking himself in the other leg. Would he never get the hang of this teenage girl thing?

"Honey, I do so care. You know that. But I can't help you fix it if you don't tell me what's wrong."

"Uncle Will, how can you say that? I don't need you to fix anything, I need–oh never mind." Lizzie pushed out of Al's arms and ran inside the house. Will's entire body jerked when the screen door slammed shut.

"Now what did I say?" He looked to his wife for answers and received a wicked smile instead. "Why are you looking at me like that?"

She stepped toward him and his heart skipped a beat. They had shared a bed with a cool wall of tension separating them. Several times he'd gone so far as to reach out to her only to be stopped by her hesitation.

Why couldn't his women understand that if they didn't tell him what was wrong he couldn't fix it?

"I think I'll deal with this on my own." She patted

his chest and walked away to leave him standing in his own puddle of melted emotions. Damn he wanted her!

Al knocked on Lizzie's door and waited for permission to enter. She found the girl laying face down in the middle of a pile of teen magazines and color brochures. "What's all this about Lizzie?"

"Jamie."

"I don't understand. I thought the two of you were doing fine."

"We were–we are. Oh this is such a mess."

"Calm down and tell me all about it."

"If I'm homecoming queen, I'll need to outshine all the other girls."

Al nodded her head in agreement.

"There's a new girl in school and she seems to have set her radar on Jamie. She's always talking to him and trying to get him to do stuff with her."

Al tried to think of something even remotely comforting to say to Lizzie, but nothing came. "You and Jamie have been together a long time."

"Yeah, but what if he doesn't feel the same about me as I do about him?"

She knew that dilemma all too well, and Allison didn't have any more answers for Lizzie than she did for herself. "Trust, Sweetie. You just have to trust what you have."

"I heard a bunch of girls talking after gym and Jill is getting some designer gown from *Neiman Marcus*. I'll look like a country bumpkin for sure."

Al sat and listened as Lizzie rambled on about the trauma bound to ruin her forever. When she'd finished, Al hugged her and promised to fix everything. "You just need the perfect dress." She spread the brochures out in front of them and pointed. "Pick one."

They spent the next hour sifting through colors, styles and matching shoes and accessories from a stack of magazines and catalogues. Several times they heard Will outside the door, but every time, he left without knocking.

When it was all said and done, Al gathered the desired designs and got up. She stopped and looked at Lizzie before she left the room. "I'll take care of everything."

"Are you sure, Al?"

"You have my word on it." Al closed the door quietly and returned to the back yard. She stepped up behind Will and gently let her hands rest on his shoulders. He immediately tensed and she hated knowing she had caused it, not Lizzie's latest crisis, but her own stubbornness.

"Is she going to live?" Will asked, his tone a bit sullen.

"I'm sure of it. But she needs you." Will tried to stand, but Al held him in place. "Not now."

"Am I ever going to understand this?" He lowered his head and rested it on his arms. "Sometimes I think she would have been better off with–"

"Don't you dare say it. Lizzie is exactly where she should be. She knows how much you love her and you are about to get a chance to prove it the only way that matters to a teenage girl."

"So when do I get to be let in on this little secret of yours?"

"Tomorrow, when we go into to the city to shop." Al waited for Will's reaction. She still chuckled every time she thought of their last adventure in shopping land.

"Oh no. I told you before that I wasn't going to do that anymore. You can't make me." He slid sideways on the bench and she scooted in next to him.

"Oh don't be such a baby. We're going to a real store and I promise, no livestock." She tucked her pink painted fingernail behind his ear and slid it down slowly. Goosebumps popped up all along his neck and down his arm. He tilted his head giving her access to his collarbone and she obliged him by tucking her hand inside his shirt.

"I don't want to go shopping."

"But this is for Lizzie. She needs you. This is your big chance to be more than Uncle Will. You get to be her father."

He turned and looked at her with tears in his eyes. "I won't ever be her father. I could never be the kind of dad Coop was."

Al understood his feelings. She couldn't imagine ever replacing Marty. Sympathizing with him, Al tucked her fingers into his hair and pulled his head toward her. "We don't have to replace them. We only have to find our own place in her heart."

Will leaned his head on her shoulder and tugged her closer against him. She didn't have the strength or the heart to refuse him. She needed his comfort and his tenderness. He turned and looked at her. "So how does my going shopping help this?"

"I'll tell you tomorrow. Right now I think we need to eat those burgers before they turn to charcoal."

When she finally slipped into bed shortly after her husband, Al was disappointed to find Will already asleep. She lay on her side next to him and watched him sleep. After tossing and turning for some time, he finally settled down facing her. The sheet had fallen between them and Al couldn't make herself cover him back up. She watched his chest rise and fall under the layer of hair and longed to run her fingertips across the defined area.

Each breath he took sent a wave of mint freshness drifting toward her. The scent tortured her with memories of his soft lips pressed against her own. Heavens how she wanted him. Anger rushed through her, anger at herself for turning a cold shoulder to him. Not only was she punishing him, but herself as well. Seeing him so vulnerable earlier had made her realize the truth. It didn't matter to her if he loved her back. He needed her and she needed him. More than anything she needed to make this family–her family–work. All of their lives depended on it.

Lizzie settled into the back seat of the Mustang,

while Al shoved Will toward the driver's side and held the door open for him. Once he'd climbed in behind the wheel, she ran around and climbed in next to him. She'd gone to the shelter early so she would have the whole day to spend shopping.

She wiggled down into the bucket seat contemplating how to tell Will the news.

"We have to buy a formal dress for Lizzie and a tuxedo for you."

She grabbed the dashboard when Will checked his rearview mirror and swung the car around and headed back the way they'd come.

"Would you be careful? What are you doing, Will?"

"I'm going home. I'm not going dress shopping and I don't need a tux."

Al sighed in complete exasperation. Was every man in America as infuriatingly hard headed as her husband? She smiled, still warmed by the way the words 'her husband' sounded to her. "Will, Lizzie is devoted to Jamie Pickett and if she is elected homecoming queen she'll be humiliated to have to dance with someone else." Al tried to sound as melodramatic as Lizzie had when relaying the tale to her.

"So she goes with Pickett. Better yet, she could not go at all. She's too young to be parading around like a piece of meat."

Al giggled aloud and he turned toward her with an unamused expression on his handsome face. "I fail to see the humor in this."

"You would." She banged on the dash with her open hand. "Pull over."

"No, we're going home."

"No, we're not. We are going to the mall to buy a formal dress for Lizzie." That got his attention. "Don't you think it's time we start acting like her parents? There's more to raising a child than fun and games."

He jerked the car to the side of the road and glared at her. "That's not fair, Allison. You know damn good and well how much I love Lizzie. So does she."

Al patted his arm in an attempt to soothe his ruffled feathers. "I know you love her, but this is so very important to her. She is in the midst of her first love and she needs a father figure to help her through it."

"But–"

"Will, no one would ever question her if you were on her arm. This is a big moment for her and I think it would be okay for you to stand in her father's place."

"I don't know, Al. Won't she feel like I'm trying to take Coop's place?"

"She thinks you won't do it."

He lowered his head and rested it against the steering wheel. "I'd do anything for her."

She turned back and looked at Lizzie who sat quietly in behind them. "Anything?" She smiled when he looked at her.

After some grumbling, a few expletives, and a good amount of whining, Will turned the Mustang around and once again headed toward town.

"I love you, Uncle Will."

Lizzie's declaration wrapped around his heart and squeezed. He couldn't imagine what he'd done to get so lucky.

Allison handed the color brochure to the sales clerk in the dress shop and waited while she checked her inventory. Al couldn't contain her excitement when they found the same dress in Lizzie's size. Will sat in the chair by the dressing rooms looking like a man about to be executed. He visibly cringed when the petite woman with flaming red hair informed him his moment had come.

Al watched as he paraded out in tuxedo after tuxedo. White didn't suit the dark maroon of Lizzie's dress. Gray made Will's skin look pale and lifeless, or perhaps it was his pouting face, she thought. She browsed around the store while he changed into the last one.

He cleared his throat behind her and she spun around to face him. Unable to stop herself she gasped and reached out for the counter beside her. His uncut dark blond hair hung down over the stiff collar of the western cut jacket. The white collar of his shirt set off his deep brown eyes. His weekend growth of stubble offered a dangerously handsome aura of mystery.

Her gaze traveled down his chest, button after button trailed down over his flat stomach. The crease of his jet-black trousers hung loose over his legs all the way down to the top of his shoes. She tried to think of something intelligent and complimentary to say to him. "Oh my." She'd been here before.

"I don't clean up so bad, huh?" The deep timbre of his voice rocked her world and she didn't even try to fight the impulse to touch him.

She swallowed against the lump in her throat and stepped toward him. She reached up and pretended to brush a piece of lint off the collar. He caught her hand in his and held it. Staring up into his devilishly intoxicating eyes, she struggled to remember how to breathe. His thumb brushed against her chin and her legs went weak. She leaned forward against the rock hardness of his chest and he supported her. You look–

"I believe you said oh my." His smug confidence disconcerted her and she caught her breath.

"Yes, I suppose I did." She took several small breaths and regained her composure before stepping away from him. "Don't let it go to your head."

He shifted from one foot to the other and smiled. "Too late for that?"

They gathered their purchases, got Lizzie settled in with the seamstress to get her dress fitted and headed for the Mustang. After they stored the packages behind the front seat Will caught her hand. "Why don't we go get some lunch?"

""I guess we could do that." Al peered in store windows as they walked through Sundance Square. They reached the Kinkade Gallery and Will nearly passed her by when she slipped inside the small shop. Several paintings caught her attention and she imagined her and Will in some of the more romantic settings.

With her mind she drew the two of them into place at the foot of the Lamplighter Bridge. She played the scene out in her head as he helped her up the step and moved to stand behind her at the top of the bridge. She leaned back against his chest as his arm slipped around her waist. The warmth of his touch through her muslin dress sparked a tingling sensation that soon whispered through her entire body. Gently, he turned her to face him and he lowered his mouth to cover hers.

The unfamiliar taste of sweet tobacco aroused her and she opened to allow him better access to deepen their kiss. He raised his hand up to caress the bare flesh at the base of her neck. His thumb traced small circles against her collarbone as she drank in the moment. She arched her body against his and thrust her fingers into his hair. Their soft kiss suddenly turned frantic and they grasped at one another silently begging for release from the sweet torture, but neither willing to pull away. The faint voices of people approaching broke the spell and she pulled away.

"Al, where are you?"

His hand on her shoulder brought a sigh from her lips. "Oh."

"Are you okay?" Will gently shook Allison. A little embarrassed he looked around at the few people in the gallery who had turned to stare when Al moaned out loud.

She blinked her eyes and looked around. "Oh my." Before Will could stop her she bolted out onto the sidewalk.

When he finally caught up to her, she refused to look at him. She lowered her head and skirted through the weekend tourists and shoppers. When they reached the corner they agreed to pizza for lunch and slipped into Uno's Pizzeria across from the Worthington Hotel.

The lunch crowd had come and gone so the waiter seated them right away. In a back corner away from everyone else, they slipped into an isolated booth. When Will sat down he found himself face to face with the building full of beds. The mere thought of Al anywhere near a bed was enough to send him in search of the closest pool of frigid water.

She'd kept him three feet farther than arms length away since their wedding and he didn't know how much more he could take. A man had needs and he needed his wife. Damn it, he wanted his wife. It wasn't unheard of.

"Did I mention I spoke to someone about some property for a new shelter?"

Oh boy. Here it comes. "That isn't necess–"

"We had a deal. You did what I asked and now I'll do my part. Tony and Katie will put up the down payment and I'm certain the money from the grooming will cover the mortgage."

"Al, there's something I need to tell–"

"It's all right. I know I was pretty upset at first, but

it isn't the end of the world. The animals will have the shelter they need and you will have your property."

"Brasselton is a prime location. There is plenty of area to develop without making you uproot the animals."

"Well, it doesn't matter. I think Tony has already put in a bid. We should know something in a couple weeks.

Will wanted to tell her that he had already found a piece of land to replace the one from Doc, but that would ruin the surprise. Hopefully Tony and Katie could keep the secret for a little while longer.

He'd sent a check to the old man and another to the representative for the other parcel of land he'd originally intended to give Al. He knew the Doc was out of town, but didn't see any problems.

By silent and mutual consent, they dropped the subject and concentrated on their pizza. Will watched her cut each piece with a knife and fork before carefully wrapping the excess cheese around her utensil and carefully lifting it to her mouth. "You're joking right?"

Al looked at him. "About?"

"Do you always eat pizza like that?" Will tugged the fork out of her hand and dropped it onto the table out of her reach.

"What are you doing? Give that back!" She reached for the fork, but he tossed it into the bucket of a somewhat shocked bus boy passing by.

"I'm going to give you a few lessons on proper

table etiquette." He picked a slice of pizza up and held it toward her.

"I can't eat that," she argued.

"Why not?" He took a bit off the end and rolled his eyes at her. "It's delicious."

"You've eaten off of it, for one thing." She crossed her arms over her chest and leaned back away from him.

Refusing to give, up he slipped over to her side of the booth, trapping her against the wall. She pushed against him, but with little true effort.

"You've had your mouth on my–"

"Enough! Don't you dare be so crude as to say that." She blushed and it pleased him to no end to know her mind was in the same place as his.

"Just work with me here, Al." He dangled the pizza in front of her, waving it back and forth. "Sure is good. The cheese is all stringy and warm. He took another bite and leaned forward to brush his lips against hers while he chewed.

"Will, people are gonna stare at us." He tucked the pizza in her mouth when she opened it to protest.

"Let them stare." When she finally took a small bite of the edge, he did the same and their lips brushed together. Her body trembled against his and he could have sworn he saw an actual spark of some kind of chemistry between them. He ignored the warning bells in his head and leaned forward against her. He covered her lips and drank in the flood of emotions drowning him. His body responded to the kiss while his mind fought off the doubt and fear. Every second that his tongue danced up against hers pulled him deeper into a place he'd rather not leave. The sound of a soft giggle pulled his attention and he pulled back.

Al's hand went to her lips and he enjoyed knowing that the pink burn in her cheeks was because of him. He touched his fingertip to her lower lip and she flicked her tongue out against it. He was totally unprepared for the tremor it sent through him.

"Al, do you think we could go home and finish this?" She tilted her head to the side and a stray beam of sunlight reflecting off the mirrored hotel caught in her eyes.

"I think we need to clear a few things up first."

"Like what?" He backed away, but didn't return to his side of the booth.

"I've tried to forget about it, but right after we got married and you thought Lizzie wasn't coming home you more or less told me it was none of my business."

"It was force of habit. You know that. I just reacted." Will toyed with the napkin in his lap, avoiding eye contact. "It's taken us both a little bit of time to get used to being a family unit."

"I understand that. I've grown to love Lizzie very much and I would do anything for her. She is as much my daughter as if had given birth to her myself."

Will couldn't help the smile. He knew beyond a shadow of a doubt at this moment that he loved Allison with all his heart. He reached out and wrapped several strands of her hair around his finger. "I get that and I feel the same way."

"You do?"

"Of course. I know you love Lizzie. I wouldn't have married you if I thought you weren't totally committed to her." *And me, I hope.*

He brushed away the tear slipping down her chin. Without taking his gaze away from her, he signaled the waiter for the check.

Once they picked up Lizzie, he would find something for her to do, and he would show his wife how much he loved her.

◀ Eleven ▶

"I hate this," Will whined. "I shouldn't have to do this."

Allison tugged on his collar and he feared for a moment she might choke him. "Be still. If I don't get this straight you'll embarrass Lizzie."

He jerked on the collar and Al smacked his hand. "It's too tight. How do you think she'll feel when I pass out half way across the gym due to lack of oxygen."

"Oh for crying out loud. Must everything be so dramatic for you?" She pushed his fingers away for the umpteenth time and straightened the button.

Dramatic? She didn't know dramatic. Will considered the changes in his life and wondered how he'd managed to survive. His bachelor status had gone to hell in a hand basket and now the ladies' man had managed to get mixed up with two women he couldn't live without.

"Will, I asked you a question."

"Of course you did." He smiled. "I just didn't hear what it was."

Allison sighed and he wanted to brush away the creases of concern marring her perfect forehead. He flicked a stray curl from over her eye and stared down at her. Sweet, lovely Allison. His Allison. He loved everything about her. He tried to think of the specific reasons, but too many ran together, forming her entire being.

"I wanted to know how long you plan on staying at the dance."

He grabbed her around the waist and tugged her up against him. The feel of her pressed against his chest left him breathless and giddy. "Why, you gonna miss me?" He leaned down toward her. His pride stung when he felt her stiffen.

He loosened his hold, but didn't let go. "What's the matter, Al?"

"Nothing."

"Sometimes I'm afraid to joke with you."

Allison sighed. "I'm sorry, but not everything is a joke."

"Why is it so hard for you to imagine us being happy?" He wished he could keep the irritation from his voice, but something snapped. "Damn it, Al. I'm not a bad guy and I didn't force you into this." He wasn't sure what he should have said, but he knew immediately that wasn't it.

She pushed away from him and stalked toward the door. "I never said you did. And I know what kind of guy you are." She slammed the door behind her, leaving him standing alone in their bedroom.

What would it take to make her understand? Suddenly, something new occurred to him. What if she truly didn't love him? That left him cold.

She was nowhere to be found when he pulled out of the driveway to meet Lizzie at the dance. Luckily, he only needed to stay long enough to escort her to the stage, and then he could take care of things with Allison.

Feeling lonely and a bit jealous, Allison watched him drive away. She'd never seen a man look so handsome in what he called a monkey suit. He looked like anything but a monkey. Every second he stood before her made her sadder. How did she think she would be able to pick up her old life where she left off when her usefulness to Will ended? She lowered her foot and swung the old hammock gently. If only she knew for sure that Will wanted to be with her.

Hoyden stirred beneath her and she reached down to scratch the beast's head. "I know girl, but they need this time alone without us."

The golden retriever stretched out with a dog-breath yawn and promptly hopped up onto the hammock. After several frantic moments, Allison steadied the swing and settled back with Hoyden planted firmly on her chest. Their usual arrangement.

The moon glistened in the sky, lending ambiance to the still evening. The small sounds of creatures sharing the night calmed her, as they always had. Croaking frogs and tweeting birds took the edge off her nervous state and left her thinking of Will and Lizzie. Her own lacking relationship with her mother made her more determined than ever to make sure

Lizzie never felt neglected for so much as a second. She deserved a good life, as did Will.

Her eyelids grew heavy as she listened to the music of the night. Within minutes she drifted off to sleep.

Several things happened at once and Allison had no time to react to any of them. Her mind registered the slamming of the back door at the same moment Hoyden decided to abandon ship. The hammock swung and flipped Allison into an extremely undignified heap on the damp ground. Her head throbbed and her muscles ached, but not as much as her pride stung at the sound of Will's laughter nearby.

"You oughta have that animal put down." She smacked the netting of the swing out of her hair as she struggled to get to her feet.

Hoyden hurried back to her side, ever quick to make amends.

Will rushed over and offered a hand to help her up. "You should be use to it by now."

At first, she hesitated, but the thought of touching him won over her inner turmoil at the same thought. The rough skin of his palm warmed the inside of her hand.

How would she ever come to terms with all this? She needed him so desperately, but couldn't find the strength to tell him.

She held her breath as he turned her hand over in his. The sensuality of his fingers tracing the lines of her palm soothing. He lifted it to his lips, but she pulled away before he could make contact.

"You really shouldn't be out here alone so late. I know you think it's safe, but–"

Allison stood. Unable to stand the closeness of their bodies any longer, Allison stepped back. "Oh stop. A prowler wouldn't stand a chance against the beast." She reached down and patted Hoyden's head, thankful for the distraction.

Will brushed some grass from her hip and the motion swept her insides into turmoil. How would she ever walk away from the man who left her feeling totally useless without him by her side?

"It's after midnight." He lifted his hand and touched her cheek with the tip of his finger. "I hate that you're angry with me," he whispered.

Her heart sped up as she leaned toward him. "I'm not upset with you. I just have a lot going on in my head."

"Is that all?"

"With the land sale and the marriage and everything Lizzie is into, I haven't had much time to consider the direction my life is heading."

"Where is that, Al?" He took her by the hand and led her to the picnic table in the center of the yard. "Sit with me."

"I should get inside."

"Lizzie is still at the dance and I want us to get some things worked out."

"Did everything go all right with Lizzie?"

"It went perfect, Al. I left her in the hands of Jamie Pickett, and he better be keeping those hands to himself."

She settled down next to him, careful not to let their bodies touch. The mere thought made her tingle.

The breeze from an approaching storm rustled the leaves and sent a chill racing along her spine. She crossed her arms over her chest and sighed. She did love the storms of Texas and tonight's promised to be a humdinger.

"I've got some things I need to do before I go to bed." Al hurried across the yard opened the door just as the phone rang. She picked it up and listened.

Then she slid to the floor.

Will grabbed for her as the telephone clattered onto the tile floor. He put the phone to his ear, but heard nothing. "Al, honey. Tell me what's wrong."

She stared for a moment then pulled him closer. "We have to go to town." A sob shook her entire body.

"What's happened? Tell me." He didn't mean to yell, but his guts twisted around and he knew something was terribly wrong.

"The car that Jamie and Lizzie were in was involved in an accident."

He dropped down next to her and pulled her into his arms. At first he thought he needed to get up and go, but he realized he needed to calm down and make sure Al was all right. He stroked her hair and held her tight for as long as he could. Finally, she pushed away from him and they both struggled to their feet.

"We have to go to her. She needs us."

"It's a mistake. I know it is."

They were almost to the car when Katie and Tony pulled up in front of the house. Al rushed into Katie's arms.

"It can't be true," Al sobbed.

"I know, Sweetie. Tony's friend from the PD called and said we might want to come get you."

"It's wrong. Lizzie is fine." Will stumbled toward the car. He ignored the small cold lump inside him and held fast to the warmth of his love for Lizzie. "I'd know if something bad had happened to Lizzie."

Will recognized several sets of parents milling around the waiting room when they got to the hospital. Jamie Pickett's father sat in a chair. A nurse struggled to get him to calm down. The old man's eyes stared blindly past them.

They went to the counter and told the nurse who they were. Several of the others turned and looked at them.

"Where's my daughter–I mean my niece?" His voice shook with barely controlled panic.

"Sir, of the three passengers in the car, two survived. Both boys' parents are already here."

"Just take me to Lizzie's room," he demanded. When no one moved he banged his fist on the counter. "Now."

A doctor wearing blood-soiled scrubs slipped up next to him and placed a hand on his shoulder. "If you'll come with me."

Will and Allison followed the older man down a series of hallways that finally ended in a large room. Allison clung to his arm as they both stared at the small body lying on the bright white sheets.

A clear plastic tent covered the upper half of her body and a mass of tubes and wires spread out in every direction. Will's body jerked with every beep of the monitors and machines keeping the young girl alive.

Together they moved toward the bed until they stood close enough to look down into the barely visible eyes of such a fragile creature. Will turned and looked at Allison and she crumbled into his arms.

"Oh dear God."

Will turned to the doctor. "Who is this? They told us our daug–Lizzie was here."

The doctor hurried forward. "I don't understand. Are you telling me this isn't your daughter?"

"Dear God no. Lizzie has brown eyes. Gloriously alive and beautifully brown eyes. I don't know who this is."

Allison hugged him so tightly she thought she might cut off her own air supply. The doctor quickly led them out of the room and shouted for the nurses milling around the waiting area.

Will pulled Al down into a chair and they clung to each other as if nothing could tear them apart. Will looked over Al's head and saw the owner of Pickett's store barely clinging to his chair. A moment later, another doctor came and informed him that Jamie would be fine. The man crumbled to the ground and wept.

Suddenly, another wave of panic flooded through Will. "If that's not Lizzie, where is she?"

Allison looked up at him as the emergency room doors slid open and Lizzie raced into the waiting area. Close on her heels followed a somber-faced Grace.

Lizzie threw herself into Will's arms and cried on his shoulder. "I didn't know what happened."

"It's okay, honey," Will soothed.

"I didn't know what to do. Some of the kids were drinking and they wanted to leave the dance. I refused to go and then Jamie convinced Greg and Jill to let him drive them home."

Allison held Lizzie's hands in her face. "Were you and Jamie drinking as well?"

Lizzie shook her head frantically. "No I swear. That's why Jamie offered to drive them home."

"So why weren't you with them?" Will asked, afraid to take his gaze off her.

Grace stepped forward and rubbed Lizzie's back. "I knew about the dance and I wanted to see Lizzie on her special night. I was outside when I saw them coming out."

"Aunt Grace offered to bring me home, so the others left without me."

Will pulled both Lizzie and Al closer against him and stared over their heads at Grace. "Thank you. I don't know how to thank you."

Grace huffed, but then backed down. "Lizzie

swears she is happy with you and she has asked me to give you the benefit of the doubt."

"I don't need you to do me any fav–"

Grace cut him off. "I have promised Lizzie that I will not interfere in your lives as long as I see that she is well cared for and loved."

"I see."

"She has assured me that she is both. I only hope that whatever happens between you and–your wife, you will remember that Lizzie always comes first."

Allison pushed against him and turned to face Grace.

"Lizzie is the most important person in the world to both of us and in spite of your meddling and lack of faith in Will, she loves you."

"And I her," Grace said softly.

"She needs you in her life as much as she needs us. If you mean what you say, I think it's time we all begin acting like a family."

Will held back for a moment, but finally nodded his agreement. "For Lizzie."

Several hours later, when they were certain everything would end well, Will and Allison took Lizzie home. They had to promise they would bring her back to the hospital to see Jamie first thing in the morning.

They rode for some time in silence before Will spoke. "Jamie told the police that Jill was so drunk and demanding Jamie pay attention to her that she grabbed the steering wheel as they took a curve."

"That's how he lost control of the car," Allison added.

"It doesn't matter as long as he's going to be okay. I couldn't bear to lose him too." Lizzie leaned over and let her head rest on Allison's shoulder the rest of the way home.

"We're all going to be okay." Will struggled to keep his eyes on the road and off his women. The time had come for everything to be settled.

◀ Twelve ▶

Brasselton had finally settled back into its usual mode. Nearly a month had passed since the tragic night of homecoming. Will had spent as much time as he could settling things into place. He'd left Allison alone as she'd set about to raising money and trying to place her small charges. Since the night of the accident they'd both been hard pressed to let Lizzie out of their sight, but she'd insisted on being by Jamie's side as often as possible to supervise his recovery.

"I'm heading over to the community center to get everything set up for the auction." Allison shouted as she hurried toward the door.

"Oh no you don't. We have something to discuss." Will tried to catch her, but she slipped out and rushed to the car.

The blasted woman had gotten away again. Since bringing Lizzie home, they'd both made every effort to strengthen their marriage. He admired her effort to make their house a home. Only one thing loomed between them. Since she wouldn't let him talk to her at home, in private, he would do what he had to.

An hour later, he stood at the back of the

community center watching his wife parade across the stage setting up small cages. When the auction finally started, he set his plan into motion.

The first animal up for bidding was Stubby. The goal of the auction was to place as many animals as possible and build up enough donations to move the remaining animals to the new shelter. He'd tried to tell Al that none of this was necessary, but the woman could be more than a little hard headed.

Minutes passed as the members of the community silently bid on the small half-tailed ferret that had managed to win its own place in his heart. When the bidding reached its peak, Will nodded. The auctioneer announced that the small rodent had been sold to the man at the back of the room.

Allison caught his gaze and her cheeks flamed.

Now he would get it for sure. "I'll pick up my new pet later." He turned to leave, hoping she would follow, but instead she bellowed from the stage.

"Wait just a minute."

He turned back and faced her like the man he was. "Yes, ma'am."

She crooked her finger at him and he found himself helpless to resist her beckoning. "This isn't funny Will Hoyt. I'm doing the only thing I can to save these animals and I expect you to back me up on this."

He smiled up at her. "Oh, I'll back you up anytime, sugar."

Several of the town's folk chuckled and she turned a melodramatic glare on them all. The room went still again.

Will turned to the back of the room when the door opened. Katie rushed forward and he took the envelope from her.

"What's this all about?" Allison demanded.

Damn she looked cute with her hands on her hips and her foot tapping.

"I have been trying to tell you for over a month. You let me know when you're ready to listen." Will turned and headed back up the aisle.

"Fine. Tell me what your little secret is."

A murmur rustled through the room and Will had to laugh. Darn near half the town knew his 'little secret' and he couldn't believe she didn't know.

"I've been trying for so long to tell you, but every time I try, you cut me off." He went to stand at her feet, leaning casually against the edge of the stage.

"I'm listening."

The soft glow in her cheeks struck something deep inside him and he wondered how he had ever survived without her. She made his life complete and he'd never had a clue anything was missing. The soft gentle curves of her body left him breathless, as did the tinkle of her voice.

"Spit it out, Wilfred."

Most of the time, he thought.

The crowd began growing restless and he knew he had to act fast before one of the garden women exploded from holding in his secret for so long. "I've been trying to tell you that you don't need to raise money to buy new land."

She looked down at him. "Well, that's just fine and dandy Will, but we've already put a bid on a lot."

"You won't get it," he stated simply.

"And why on earth not? You think you're the only business person in this town who can wheel and deal for land?"

He laughed out loud.

"When I want something I know exactly what to do to get it."

"Yes, you do darlin'," he teased. He remembered several of the more recent nights when hours at the work site had left him exhausted. She'd made it perfectly clear that she had wants and needs and he was darn well going to take care of them. Not that he minded making love with his wife until all hours of the night and many mornings.

She leaned down and swatted at him. "Stop that. I fully intend to do whatever it takes to get my animals where they belong."

"I see." He held the envelope out in front of him and turned it over several times.

She reached down and tried to snatch it away from him. He jerked it away and everyone laughed.

"What is that? And why do you look so proud of yourself."

Will couldn't help himself. If he wasn't careful she was gonna wipe the, *God I love my wife,* look right off his face. "This is my wedding present to you."

That stopped whatever nicety was about to flow

from her sweet and oh so kissable lips.

"That's right. I got you a present. Now don't you feel bad about being so mean to me in front of all our friends?" He poked his lip out and pretended to be hurt.

"I don't understand what this is all about," she said softly. "Maybe we should go somewhere and discuss this in private."

He held his hand up. "Oh no you don't. You made the rules this time." He handed her the packet of papers. "Look at them."

Allison took the envelope and pulled out two more envelopes. She opened the first one and unfolded the sheets. "It's the deed to the land we put a bid on for the new shelter. Your name is on it." She folded it back up and stuffed it back into the envelope.

"Yes it is."

She shoved the papers toward him and did all she could to hold her temper in check. How could he be so insensitive? First he'd bought the shelter property, now he had swooped in and all but stolen the other land she'd worked so hard to find. "How could you?"

He lowered his head and shook it back and forth several times. "Will you never learn?"

"Learn what?" she asked. "That whatever Will wants, Will gets," she mocked.

She turned to walk away from him, but he caught her ankle gently in his hand.

"Not so fast. There's more."

He pushed the packet back toward her, but she

refused to take it. Suddenly, from the back of the room she heard Katie's voice. "Take it, Allie."

Slowly, Allison took the packet.

"Open it. I want you to look inside the other envelope."

Her hands trembled as she pulled the other sheet out and opened it up. Tears welled up in her eyes as she stared down at the second deed.

"Oh for the love of Mike. I didn't mean for you to cry."

Will climbed up onto the stage and pulled her into his arms.

"I saw the other deed and—"

"Yes, once again sugar, you assumed the very worst of me. When will you ever learn?"

"I've learned one thing."

"What's that?" he asked.

"I've learned that falling in love with you has given me a chance to be happy. I was just so confused."

"You love me?"

She gazed up into her husband's eyes and smiled. "Of course I do. I think I have from the very first. I was just so afraid you didn't have room in your life for me."

"I feel like such a fool. All this time I've been assuming that—"

Allison smiled. "I think it's time we base this marriage on something other than assumptions."

"That's a fact, darlin'."

* * *

One month later, Allison once again stood in front of the entire community of Brasselton.

Since Will had given her the deed to the land, they had settled into their marriage with a comfortable sense of belonging. Allison scanned the room, hoping to see Will, but her refusal to let him help with the settling of the details concerning the grand opening of the shelter had left him a bit irritable. With a final scan of the room and the entrances, Allison nodded to the mayor, signaling him to begin.

Will stumbled into the room with all the grace of a charging rhino. He tripped over a small furry animal lying sprawled across the floor. He glanced around the room, scanning the crowd for his wife. When he spotted her his heart flip-flopped in his chest.

He looked directly to the left and saw Lizzie sitting next to a young man in a rock and roll T-shirt. The boy never took his eyes off Lizzie.

"Can I have your attention, please?" Jacob Millsap, the newly elected mayor of Brasselton stepped up onto the makeshift podium and tapped his glass on the wood. "I'd like to take this opportunity to welcome y'all to the dedication ceremony of the Happy Home for Wayward Strays."

Will couldn't stop the smile tugging at his lips when the man stumbled over the name of the building. He'd argued for days with Al, Lizzie, and Katie about it, but in the end, three beautiful women won. Nothing new in his life.

Of course, he hadn't argued very hard, just a token fight to keep the women on their toes.

"I'd like to give the floor to Allison Hoyt, the owner and operator of the new facility. Everyone in the room applauded while several dogs barked in unison with the clapping.

"Thank you," Allison said as she moved behind the podium. "There was a time not too long ago when I thought that maybe all of these sweet little animals would be homeless. A man came into town and threatened to take their home away. At first I didn't know what to do, but then I realized I would do whatever it took to see that it didn't happen."

"Did you really think you had to marry him to keep it?" someone teased from the crowd.

"Well, Mr. Cramer, loyalty leads one down strange avenues."

Will winked at his wife. Anyone else might have taken her seriously, but he'd gotten used to her rapier wit and sharp remarks.

"When I found out my husband had other plans for this property, I was less than thrilled, but after some work, I made him see how important it is for everyone and everything to have a place to belong."

The crowd applauded and Will knew the truth of her words. He'd never really belonged anywhere but with her. How on earth a rag tag crew of misfit animals had shown him that was still out of his realm of understanding, but they had. The strays had grown to be as much a part of his life as Al and Lizzie.

Will glanced back over at Lizzie just as her friend leaned over and kissed her. Will's eyes popped wide open and he moved toward them without a clue as to what he intended to do.

The sound of his wife's voice stopped him.

"If my husband would join me on the stage–now, we'll get on with the real reason were here today."

He stopped and glanced back and forth between Lizzie and Al. She had him again. If he didn't get some control over the women in his life, Lizzie would be married and moving out and he'd be henpecked, worse than he already was.

The crowded room filled with the sound of catcalls and whistles as he wrapped his arms around his wife's waist.

"I know a lot of you don't know my husband very well, but I know once you do he'll become as special to you as he is to me and Lizzie."

Will looked down at her, his face a shade brighter from embarrassment.

She smiled and continued. "We are dedicating this shelter to the memory of his sister." The crowd sat silent. "Like my husband here, I have been assured that Marty would never turn a stray away, no matter how pathetic it was. She had a heart of gold and I know she would have been honored to be a part of something so special."

Will's eyes filled with tears and he made no effort to hide the love shining in his face. For a moment, he simply stared down at her. Several times he opened his mouth to speak, but closed it without saying anything. Finally, he found his voice.

"I never imagined I could love you anymore than I did a minute ago, but now I can't even find the words to tell you what this means to me." He turned and smiled at Lizzie who sat off to the side wiping tears from her cheeks and beaming with pride.

First one person clapped, then another, until the entire of the crowd joined in. Finally, the crowd settled down and they concluded the ceremony.

Will was about to step down when a voice from the crowd called out to him.

"Hey there, any truth to the rumor Brasselton is about to get a new misfit?"

Will looked around, curious about why the question was directed at him.

"Well, thanks, Katie; I hadn't had a chance to fill him in on that yet." Al turned in her husband's arms and looked up at him. Blank confusion melted into pure joy when she moved his hand down to rest on her stomach again. "We're gonna start our own shelter for misfits in about six months."

His mouth took hers in a soul-searing kiss that shook her to the very root of her existence. After the crowd stopped applauding, he lifted her up into his embrace and swung her around. "Even as much as I love you, I reckon there will always be enough love for one more misfit. A misfit sure to be as beautiful and incredible as his mother."

"His?" Al teased.

"Lord help me, I don't think I could handle another woman. We'll have to open a chain of shelters."

"Would that be so bad?"

Will smiled at her. "Not as long as you were always right there by my side to do it."

"Always."

Allison snuggled deeper into her husband's embrace as the room once again echoed with applause.

A commotion at the back of the room caught her attention and several of the men stepped aside. Before Allison knew what was happening, the ball of golden fur came barreling toward her.

She turned her head and caught sight of Katie rushing toward them. "Grab that dog!"

Before anyone could react Allison yelled, "Stop."

Hoyden slid to a stop and nearly plowed into their legs. "Not this time, princess," Allison added.

Will laughed. "I must be in heaven. I've found a woman who can control my dog."

Allison kissed him square on the mouth. "And don't you ever forget it."

The End

Karen L. Syed is the president and COO of Echelon Press, LLC. Every day is a new success story for her as she continues to grow herself and her business. She has seen seven of her own novels published (writing as Alexis Hart), along with numerous articles and short stories. As a former bookstore owner, she garnered a nomination from Publishers Weekly for their Bookseller of the Year award. She is committed to helping and encouraging everyone she comes in contact with to seek a healthier and more positive quality of life by reaching for their dreams.

Her newest fascination has taken root in the Steampunk industry. This tremendously interesting genre based in the Victorian era is helping to feed a minor obsession with the time period. She is currently embarking on her own Steampunk series called *Petticoat Junction*. With more than a quarter of a century experience in the book industry, she hopes this one will propel her into the bestseller category. Time will tell.

You can learn more about Karen Syed at http://klsyed.com.

www.ingramcontent.com/pod-product-compliance
Lightning Source LLC
Chambersburg PA
CBHW072230170626
46813CB00003B/1152

* 9 7 8 1 5 9 0 8 0 8 5 6 6 *